VE

MAIDSTONE

6/11

Please return on or before the latest date above.
You can renew online at *www.kent.gov.uk/libs*
or by telephone 08458 247 200

CHARTER MARK

CUSTOMER SERVICE EXCELLENCE   **Libraries & Archives**

Kent County Council

00884\DTP\RN\07.07   LIB 7

CAIN BRAND

CAIN BRAND

by

Craig Campbell

Dales Large Print Books
Long Preston, North Yorkshire,
BD23 4ND, England.

British Library Cataloguing in Publication Data.

Campbell, Craig
    Cain Brand.

A catalogue record of this book is
available from the British Library

ISBN 1-84262-269-2 pbk

Published in Large Print 2003 by arrangement with
Robert Hale Ltd.

Dales Large Print is an imprint of Library Magna Books Ltd.

Printed and bound in Great Britain by
T.J. (International) Ltd., Cornwall, PL28 8RW

1

Rough Justice

By one o'clock in the afternoon, the tall thunderheads which had been building massively on the southern horizon, began to sweep in until they covered the entire sky, grey here and there, but mostly black and threatening. The rain began fifteen minutes later, sweeping down in vast sheets, driven by the wind that had lifted with the coming of the storm, striking viciously at the pines and cedars which hugged the edges of the rocky gradients. Lightning flared, lancing across the beserk heavens, followed almost at once by the vicious roll of thunder, sending great booming echoes beating back from the tall hills that lay on either side of the trail.

Ross Halloran drilled his heels into the flanks of his mount, set it into the wind, bowing his own head as he leaned forward in the saddle, the thunder roaring in his ears, the rain slashing violently at his face whenever he lifted it momentarily to stare at the winding trail ahead of him. Again and again, visible through the thrashing branches of the trees overhead, the lightning flared in wicked, whip-like streaks, forking among the scudding clouds, followed by the bucketing rumble of the thunderclaps. There was savagery in the scene, frightening, yet strangely beautiful. This, thought Halloran, was Nature in the raw, how it must surely have been on the morning following Creation, when the world lay at the beginning of its history.

Reining up on a wide ledge that looked down into the narrow, but deep, valley below, he saw that the river, normally sluggish and slow-moving where it ran through the wide channel it had carved out for itself over the long centuries, was now a raging, thundering torrent, running deep and fast. Giving a quick look to the south, and seeing no break in the storm, he cast his mind ahead, wondered whether he would be able to ford the river when he reached the point where the trail dipped out of the hills and entered the valley where it widened out some five miles ahead.

Fingering the few coins in his pocket, staring down at the tattered grey uniform he wore, he wondered too what might lie ahead of him. The war was over, the bitter rift which had divided a nation was healed; at least on the surface, but there were few who really believed that it would be healed for many years, possibly decades, to come. The men who had fought in the Confederate Army were particularly bitter. Ross Halloran was one of them. The legacy of hatred that had been born, and nurtured during the long years of battle, showed in his eyes and the set of his face. The red, savage swirl of battle still existed in his mind and the cruel, merciless task of staying alive which had been the prime consideration during those years just past, was something he could not throw off.

Restlessness bubbled in him and even the thought that he was going home, that another day would see him there, after all those years, failed to bring a sense of ease to his mind. Things would not go easy for the South, now that the war was ended. They were a defeated people. The Yankees would ride in and take everything, strip their lands of food and cattle.

Shivering, he pulled up the collar of his tunic. The swaying branches over his head dripped a continual rain of heavy drops on to his head and even though they broke the full fury of the storm, they afforded little protection from the rain.

Stepping down from the saddle, he tightened the worn cinch under the horse, stood for a moment to give it rest, trying to push his sight through the wall of rain and darkness. Beside him, the horse, its coat glistening with the rain, stood patient and quiet, bunching its shoulder muscles at times, nuzzling up to him as he ran his hand over its bowed neck.

Rubbing the rain from his eyes, he swung back into the saddle. His clothing, completely sodden now, clung to his body, chafing his skin with every movement he made. At least, he told himself, he was among the hills. Had the storm hit a day earlier, it would have caught him out in the treeless plain which he had just crossed, where the trail cut arrow-straight across the glaring white alkali, little more than a dusty ribbon of ploughed-up dirt, cut into the sun-baked ground by the hoofs of thousands of horses which had gone over it since the trail had first been blazed many years before.

There was no illusion in his mind as to what he would find when he reached the ford. A swirling wall of water, rushing over the rocky bed, several feet higher than usual at this season, carrying down huge logs, smashing them against the upthrusting boulders, making a crossing highly dangerous. Hunching his shoulders forward as the dampness soaked into his bones, feeling the weariness from the long journey eat into his aching bones, he wheeled away from the lip of the smooth ledge, took the trail that wound deeper into the trees, a lonely man heading into an unknown destiny, unknowing as yet of the forces which were to be brought to bear on him in the very near future shaping his entire life.

By the time he came within sight of the ford, the storm was blowing itself over. There were wide streaks of bright blue to the west and as he came down from the timberline, the sun came out, bright and glaring in his eyes so that he was forced to squint against it through narrowed lids. The rain stopped and the ground and trees steamed as the growing heat brought the moisture out in a swirling white mist. He walked his mount to the river bank, sat easy in the saddle, contemplating the great angry rush of the water. The river had risen tremendously due to the storm. Great plumes jetted high into the air where the current struck the rocks out near the middle of the river. The sweeping, muddy water, had already eaten deeply at the soft earth of the banks, carrying soil and stones downstream. There was white, foaming water in the narrows perhaps thirty yards upstream where high rocks crowded in on the banks; a bubbling, frothing, boiling wall of water which threatened to carry everything before it. Tree trunks, swept down from the higher levels, were visible at intervals in the water, tumbling end over end in a mad, chaotic confusion.

Turning his mount, he walked it along the bank, keeping away from the edge where the soil was continually crumbling away, until he reached a point where the river was wider than at the ford, not quite as deep, but still dangerous. The horse bent its head, seemed unsure of itself, pawing at the ground nervously. Bending forward, Ross ran his hand along its neck, speaking softly and soothingly to it. There was another moment while he considered, then he put the horse into the swirling water. The slower current near the bank caught at the horse, the water swirling around its legs as it moved further into midstream.

Thirty yards and the bottom fell away abruptly, the horse began to swim and Ross eased himself smoothly from the saddle, clinging to the bridle, as he let the horse pull him along, fighting the current, but allowing it to carry them downstream a little way. There was no point in trying to strike straight across the river even at its widest point. To have tried to do so would have meant using up all of the horse's reserves of strength, giving it little chance of reaching the other side. Fifty yards and Ross's feet caught on something. A moment later, the horse floundered up beside him on the sandbar which was submerged now beneath the surface of the water. Thinking back, Ross recalled this stretch of smooth sand which was normally visible when the river was at its usual level. Odd, he thought, how little things like that tended to slip from the memory, requiring something to jog the mind to bring them back again.

Across the sandbar, and then they were in deeper water once more, with the current striking at them, carrying them further downstream so that they were moving diagonally over the river. The further bank seemed to be moving past them at a blurring, alarming speed, but Ross knew that it would be dangerous to try to force the horse to change its course through the surging water. Somehow, they made the further bank, clambering up through the shallows on to dry land. While he gave his mount chance to blow, Ross built himself a cigarette with slow deliberation, fumbled for a lucifer in his pocket and lit the smoke, inhaling deeply. He was wet and uncomfortable, but he had endured more physical discomfort than this during the war, and he immediately dismissed it from his mind. He still had another fifty or sixty miles to cover before he reached the ranch and he knew there would be another camp, somewhere in the hills, before he tasted any of the home comforts he had known before he had ridden away to the war.

Darkness found him riding across the vast plain that stretched away south of the hills. The storm seemed to have swept the air clear of dust and the stars were hard and brilliant, standing out in their thousands across the vast, inverted bowl of the heavens, so close that, squatting near the fire he had built, it seemed he had only to stretch up to be able to touch them with his hand. Around him, the great eternal stillness of the plains was a tangible thing that could be felt. It reached out from the far horizons on every side of him, holding him fast in a web which could not be broken, and the tiny orange glow thrown out by his fire, seemed to be imprisoned in the great darkness of the night.

In spite of the deep solitude, he felt no concern. All of his days, ever since he could remember, had been made up of a pattern of plains and hills, of sun-burned days and the pale moonlit nights, of silence and warmth and cold. He placed his blanket close to the fire, just inside the rim of light, then finished the second cup of hot coffee, smoked a last cigarette slowly, checked his mount, and went back to the fire, dropping another handful of twigs on to it before sliding into his blankets, stretching himself out on the ground, hands clasped behind his neck, staring up at the night sky over him.

Far off in the distance, he thought he heard a faint sound; little more than a muted echo. But there was no repetition of it even though he strained his ears to catch the slightest sound and, turning over on to his side, he slept.

When he woke, it was almost dawn. To the east, the sky was streaked with grey, but over to the west, it was still dark and the last stars were just visible as he got to his feet, rolled up his blankets and built up the fire, blowing on the red embers to bring it to life again. He ate a hurried breakfast, a sense of urgency rising in him now, saddled up and rode out of the shallow depression where he had made his camp. They passed through a rugged stretch of country, a land of rising buttes and mesas, where the great red sandstone rocks had been etched and fluted by long geological ages of wind and dust storms, fashioned into twisted figures of strange, eerie beauty. In the distance, still low on the skyline, the blue hills lifted in the first glimmerings of daylight, standing out in soft contours against the harsh lines of the desert.

It was high noon by the time he crossed the plain and his mount blew its relief when its feet left the harsh grainy desert and moved up on to the soft green cushion of grass that stretched across the foothills. Unbidden, it quickened its pace, stretching into a steady lope which carried them closer to the hills. The pass which led through them now showed clearly where the rounded shoulders crowded down on the narrow trail. A mile through the pass lay the ranch where he had been born and had spent his boyhood. Not until the war had claimed him, had he ever left that place. Now he was going back, uncertain of what he would find there. Although this part of the territory had not been touched by the actual battles which had been fought during the Civil War, the last letter he had received from his father had spoken of the Yankee carpetbaggers who had been moving in on this rich territory, staking out claims for themselves, generally riding roughshod over the folks who had lived there for generations. He sincerely hoped that nothing like that had happened to his own family.

Pondering on this, he felt depressed, unusually alone and curiously vulnerable. Just because he had heard that the Yankees were in the territory was no reason for him to start jumping to conclusions, of shying away at shadows, he told himself fiercely. The South may have been beaten, but somewhere, there had to be a chance for them to rebuild something better than that which had gone before.

Rounding a bend in the trail, he hesitated as he came upon the hump of a rock outcrop. There was a side trail, leading off that on which he had been riding. For a moment, he leaned forward, staring at the other, where it wound away into the stunted bushes, finally stopping in front of an adobe building, evidently a nester's homestead. There was thin, bright wire stretched between posts which had clearly been hammered securely into the hard earth and, just beyond the wire, fronting the house, a patch of ground that had been broken by a hoe and planted with corn and alfalfa.

By heart a cattleman, he did not like the idea of men coming into this territory and squatting in these places, stringing up their wire across the range. As far as he had always been concerned, the range was meant to be open, was meant to feed the herds of longhorn cattle which would eventually, it was hoped, provide food for the hungry millions back East, and money for the people of Texas and Alabama. It was the only way in which the South could ever get back on to its feet again after the disastrous war which had just ended.

Wiping the dust from his face with his kerchief, he moved his mount forward until it came up against the wire where it stopped, turning its head to look inquiringly at him. The well-kept plots of ground spoke of hard work on the part of the family here. Grudgingly, he was forced to admit that it took a lot of guts to throw up everything they might have back East and come out here, building a place for themselves in this wilderness. The lowing of a cow at the rear of the house caught his attention and he turned to glance in that direction, saw the door of the house open suddenly and knew that he had been watched for some time. The woman who stood there held a rifle in her hands, pointing it at him as she walked forward. There was a fearless look on her face and her eyes were grey and challenging as she laid her gaze directly on him.

'Were you looking for somebody?' she asked. Her eyes narrowed a little as she lowered her gaze, allowing it to wander over the dusty, tattered uniform. Then a faint smile touched the edges of her lips. 'You may find that it isn't wise to continue wearing that colour, even here. There are many who resent it and others who may ridicule it, and from the look of you, I'd say you were a man who would not take kindly to ridicule, no matter from whom it came.'

He shrugged his shoulders. 'This is the colour I wore during the fighting.' he said quietly. 'I wore it because I like it, because I believe in what it stands for.'

'What it stood for, you mean,' she corrected him. The gun was still pointed at him, although the barrel had lowered a little. 'Are you hungry?'

He shook his head. 'I've only a little way to go now. Through the pass. But I saw this trail and I was curious. I don't remember anybody bein' here when I left.'

'We've been here for more than two years now,' she said. 'It's a hard life, but so far we've been left alone.'

'Aren't you afraid that the Yankees will move in?' he asked.

'They aren't interested in little people like us. They only want the big ranchers. Already, they're moving in. There were some heading this way three days ago, moving through the pass yonder.'

Ross felt a sudden tightness in him, but only the thinning of the lips and the white-knuckled grip on the reins gave any outward sign of this. 'Thanks for that information, Ma'am,' he said, backing his mount a little way. 'Guess I'd better be ridin' along.'

She lowered the gun, gave him a faint smile, watched as he wheeled his mount and rode back to the fork in the trail. His keen eyes brightened speculatively as he rode on towards the Pass. The wind, sweeping down from the high ridges was cool and fresh against his sunburned face. It tasted clean and sharp on his tongue, full of the aromatic smell of the green pines.

Midway through the afternoon, he rode through the pass with the towering walls of rock looming high on either side of him, the metallic echoes of his mount's hoofbeats on the hard, flint surface echoing back at him, bouncing from the stone. Landmarks were now familiar to him, this was the country he had known for more than nineteen years before he had been forced to leave and fight for the South. Now he was returning to it as one of a defeated Army, and for a Texan that was the most difficult thing to bear. The war had been over for almost three months and in that time, he had heard many of the stories of what was happening down here in this vast state. Of a tremendous land that was starving slowly but surely, preyed on by the Yankee carpetbaggers, with the great herds roaming wild and loose over thousands of square miles of worthless country. There was greatness here if only they could be left alone to find it and there were men who believed that the salvation of the whole country might be found in Texas. But such men were few and there seemed to be none of them in Congress in Washington. Any pleas fell on deaf ears. The Government of

America appeared to be only a bunch of dreamers who had no idea of how to run a country. They were out of touch with things, and were simply content to allow the rot to go on, without lifting a finger to prevent it. The prospectors, the slick dealers were making fortunes while Texas slowly died.

He put his horse to the downgrade, felt the slackening of it, but made no attempt to increase its pace, even though impatience and urgency were growing in him. The sun had drifted over to his right now, was no longer shining directly into his eyes and as he came over a lip in the trail, he stared down on to the edge of the spread.

The perimeter wire was still there, stretched across between wooden posts, hammered firmly into the ground, rusted a little now from wind and rain, but unbroken. He examined it carefully as he rode along it, noticing that it was still intact although it had evidently not been checked for some time. But what troubled him most was the fact that as far as he could see there were no cattle grazing there. When he had left, there had been a herd of close on two thousand head. Surely they could not all have strayed, not with the wire in place like this, and although they would have undoubtedly have had to sell off a few for food and other essentials, two thousand head had been a lot.

He reached the opening in the wire, went through, stringing it up behind him. The stillness was oppressive now, a feeling of trouble which he could not throw off. He sensed there was a difference about the place now, something which had not been there when he had left it. He motioned his horse to an easy canter and headed for the house, which lay just over the low hill. He was halfway there when he saw the lone rider heading towards him from a narrow belt of timber. As the horseman drew closer, Ross saw that he carried a rifle. Ross reined in to a walk, kept his hand close to the butt of the heavy revolver at his waist, a little unsure of himself, not recognizing the man.

The rider swept in close. He was a red-haired, thick-set man of average height, with a high-bridged, out-jutting nose and pale blue eyes that regarded Ross with a hostile suspicion. He slewed his horse to a halt beside the other, the rifle trained on Ross's chest, apparently accidentally, but clearly he meant to use it if he had any reason to do so.

Tightening his lips, Ross snapped: 'You got a boot for your weapon, mister?'

The man gave a quick nod. His gaze fell

towards the heavy weapon near the other's right hand.

'Then I reckon you'd better put it where it belongs.'

For a long moment, the other hesitated. Evidently this was not what he had expected. He let an appraising glance travel over Ross's uniform and what he saw evidently reassured him a little. He thrust the rifle out of sight, leaned forward with the hands crossed on the pommel.

'You wouldn't be Ross Halloran, would you?'

'That's right.' Ross gave a brief nod. He twisted his lips into a grimace of surprise. 'What's goin' on around here? Who are you, anyway?'

'The name's Faro – Will Faro. I came to work here just under a year ago. Things have been bad since then, real bad.'

'What sort of trouble?' Ross asked tautly.

'Yankees mostly. Ridin' in and takin' the best steers in the herd. They claimed they was takin' 'em to test for Texas fever, reckoned that there had been outbreaks of it due to our herds mixin' with theirs when they was driven across the border.'

'So that's how they operate,' muttered Ross under his breath. There was no such thing as Texas fever. It was all a trick to take their cattle without giving payment. Maybe they had some framed-up law to back their play. Maybe it was going on all over Texas. One of the ways the Yankees meant to use to see that the South never regained its former importance and prosperity. He felt the slow anger begin to burn inside him. Gritting his teeth, he rode forward, Faro gigging his mount, riding beside him.

'If you've got ideas about tryin' to fight these men, forget 'em,' warned the other harshly. 'I know that's easy for me to say. I don't own any of this land or these cattle. But you don't have a chance against 'em. They say they have the law behind 'em and if you try to resist, they get a warrant out from the nearest sheriff and bring a posse out to the ranch to take what they want by force.'

'And this has happened often?'

The other nodded, his face serious. 'Too often. There's less than five hundred head of beef left now. And with little enough food for 'em.'

'Seems I came back just in time.' said Ross grimly.

'You can't do anythin' to stop 'em. Unless you want to try to fight the law.'

Ross narrowed his eyes, his face tight. 'Maybe if that's the only way, then I'll have to do it.'

Faro took a sideways look at the grim-visaged man in the grey uniform who rode beside him, shook his head a little wonderingly. He had heard several other men say these same things, express the same feelings, but they had never succeeded. Was there anything about this man which marked him out as being different from the rest? Inwardly, he wasn't sure. Here was a man who had seen violence, a man who had fought in the tangled thickets of the Wilderness when Lee had almost beaten the Yankees. A man who had lived with death. Faro did not doubt that it had bred hatred and a grim determination into the other. Whether these qualities would be sufficient to stand up to the troubles which were now facing everyone in the South, he did not know.

Ten minutes later, they reined up in front of the long, low-roofed building. There was a frightening stillness about the place. Tying his horse to the hitching rail, he went in through the open ranch door and called out. The parlour was empty, but a moment later, the door to the kitchen opened and his mother came in, stood in the open doorway for a moment, staring at him in surprise, as though unable to believe her eyes.

'Ross. It really is you.' She ran forward, threw her arms around him, as though still unable to believe that he was really there. 'We didn't expect you for a week or more. How did you manage to get here so soon?'

'Rode most of the time,' he said quietly. He looked down at her, saw the lines in her face which had not been there when he had left. She seemed to have aged almost twenty years.

'I'll get you something to eat. You must be famished. Will, put my son's horse in the stable.'

'Yes, Mrs Halloran.' The other nodded, went out, and Ross seated himself at the table, glad of the opportunity to stretch out his legs and relax his taut muscles. He sat quite still for a few moments, then built himself a smoke, got to his feet and stood in the kitchen doorway while his mother bent over the stove, mixing batter in one of the bowls from the shelf.

For a long moment, neither of them spoke, then Ross said softly: 'What has been happenin' around here, mother, since I've been away? I spoke to one of the homesteaders on my way here. She told me that the Yankees were movin' in, takin' the best beef under some pretext or another, ruining us.'

She tried to speak calmly. 'All Texas is becoming an empty country. They ride in, take what they want, and then leave without offering any payment for what they take. Or if they do, it's not more than a quarter of what the cattle or horses are worth.'

'And you haven't been able to fight them. That's it, isn't it?'

She nodded, her head bent over the bowl. 'How could we fight them. Most of the men went to fight in the war. Those who were left were old and feeble. Besides, we're a conquered people now. They claim they have the law behind them, they sometimes ride in with a marshal or a sheriff, and a posse backing them up. What could we do against that?'

Yes, thought Ross bitterly; *what could they do? These men were robbing the South of everything, doing it under the guise of the law. Whether it was a law passed by misguided men in Congress, or one made up by themselves to suit their own ends, mattered little. Only those who stood in thick with the Union soldiers at the various forts along the southern trails, would get all of the supplies they needed and protection from the land-grabbing, cattle-grabbing robbers from the North.*

He squinted hard at her. 'Now that I'm back it's going to be different,' he said baldly. 'I lost far too many years fighting for something I believed to be right, to have everything taken away by these men, no matter how they pretend they have the law on their side.'

'How can you fight them?' asked his mother, a trace of bitter resignation in her tone.

'With this, if it's necessary,' he said, motioning with his thumb to the gun at his side. 'It seems to be the only real law around here now.'

2

Day of Retribution

It was an hour before noon when Ross Halloran rode across the narrow ford and entered the long, low meadow that bordered the ranch. During the three days which had elapsed since he had come riding home from

31

the war, he had been forced to assimilate the bitter knowledge that the South was dying, slowly in places, more swiftly in others, stifled by Congress and robbed by the money-grabbers who had moved in on the heels of the victorious armies of the North.

So far, he had seen nothing of these men, but there was evidence aplenty of their having been in the territory. The stock on the ranch had dwindled to less than five hundred head of cattle, including all of the mavericks that had been brought in. If things went on like this, they would have virtually nothing in a few more years. Angrily, he thought of everything his father had done in those early years to build up this ranch and everything on it, the sacrifices which had been made, the long, hard winters and the summers of drought which they had somehow survived. Then had come the war, his father dying in that first year he had been away, his mother struggling to keep things on for his sake.

The ford was wide and shallow at this spot, the water, sparkling in the flooding sunlight, running fast over the smooth sandy bottom. Here and there, the banks were bordered by clumps of tall sycamore and cedar and he dismounted to give his horse a drink before riding on to the ranch. It was a quiet, restful spot and he seated himself on his haunches on the river bank, rolling a smoke, building the neat, brown-paper cigarette with smooth, deft movements of his fingers. Lighting it, he enjoyed the first, long draw, watched the way the horse drank, with its muzzle pushed all the way below the surface of the water. His mount was a thoroughbred, drank as all thoroughbreds drank and it did him good to see it.

A sudden movement upstream caused him to turn his head sharply, his right hand reaching down for the gun at his waist. For a long moment, he could see nothing for the trees and the thickly tangled brush. Then he heard the faint bawling of cattle in the distance, heard the splashing once more and got lithely to his feet, moving back into the brush, drawing the horse with him. Jerking his gun from its holster, he tossed the half-smoked cigarette into the water and settled back to wait. The river here provided the boundary between their spread and that which belonged to Jeb Wellow, and it was just possible that some of Jeb's men were driving part of their herd down to the water. But it would be safer to wait a while under cover, to make sure of what was happening before he made a move to show himself.

He saw the first steer move out from the trees on the far side, about a hundred yards upstream, move uncertainly into the water and stand there, bawling for a moment. There was vague movement behind it among the tangled brush and a few moments later, he heard the high-pitched yelling of men urging the cattle forward. Edging his way through the undergrowth, he reached a point where he could see directly across the river. On the far bank, there was a mass of tumbled rock which lifted for almost twenty feet beyond the thin fringe of trees and among the rocks he saw perhaps fifty head or so of cattle, milling around, striving to break back up the slope, rather than move down to the water. Pulling the horse well back under cover, he looped the reins around a low branch, then eased his way forward until he was crouched down within two feet of the river bank, with only a thin layer of intertwined branches between him and the water.

He caught the brand of the cattle through the swirling cloud of dust lifted high into the still, breathless air by the milling hooves. Several belonged to Wellow, but here and there he spotted their own brand. These were evidently some of the cattle which had been hazed off the two spreads during the past week or so. Clearly they had been moved into some narrow valley on the edge of the two ranches where they were unlikely to be found and now they were being moved out, possibly to join up with others that had been taken, before being shipped out to one of the railheads.

He saw half a dozen men riding with the cattle. Four of the men were now in the water, working the reluctant beasts against the current. For a moment, Ross debated whether to try to take them all, before they could recover from their surprise at a sudden attack, then decided against it. There were too many for him to have any hope of killing or badly wounding them all, even shooting them down from ambush.

The small herd headed slowly downstream, splashing through the water, moving towards a gap in the trees where a smooth, rock escarpment ran away into the desert beyond the river. A score of longhorns began to mill stupidly in the middle of the river, lifting their lean heads as they bawled their deep-throated protests. Then they began to run as the men moved in behind them, yelling fiercely. Moving up into the rocks, they poured in a wave of solid muscle and flesh over the smooth plateau and down the other side in the direction of the desert. Ross waited tensely until the last of the men had vanished, then slipped through the trees, back to his mount, urged it out into the stream and climbed swiftly into the saddle, riding through the foaming water where it had been churned up by the herd and into a narrow gulch that opened up on one side of the plateau.

Head bent low over the saddle, he sent the horse forward, but with the din of the herd ahead of him and the steep walls of the gully closing in on both sides, there was little fear of him being heard or seen. The bottom of the gulch was dry, the ground baked hard by the sun, with long cracks streaking the surface. It veered to the left and then began to open up, breaking up into tall boulders and loose rocks around which he was forced to edge his mount at a slower, more careful pace. But there was still plenty of cover for him among the upthrusting boulders.

The yells of the men told him that they had stopped directly ahead of him and he slid from the saddle, pulling the rifle from its boot, checking that it was cocked as he slithered forward, keeping his head low, diving for the cover of a dense clump of scrub. His eyes became venomous as he watched the men moving around the milling herd. They had brought it along into a wide, but shallow, depression and three of them had dismounted, were building a fire.

Two were still in the saddle, urging the reluctant steers into a circle. There was no sign of the other, and Ross searched intently, knowing that he might be in danger until he discovered the whereabouts of that sixth man. He might at that very moment, be working his way up behind him, ready to take him by surprise.

Leaving the horse out of sight, he edged around to his left. His movements became more wary now. On one side of him a wall of rock with out-thrusting abutments protected him from being seen by anyone along the gully. He was still inwardly troubled by the fact that he had been unable to spot that sixth man. It could be that the other had ridden out, scouting ahead of the herd, but somehow, he doubted that, since there would have been too little time in which the other could have moved ahead out of sight from the low ridge near the edge of the gully.

Glancing up, to where the sunlight was reflected from the smooth rock of the cliff wall beside him, he noticed the narrow trail by which it would be possible for him to climb to the top, thereby bringing him out above these men. Moving forward, he had climbed a couple of feet when he froze instantly. The faint smell of tobacco smoke reached his nostrils. Very carefully, he lowered himself down to the floor of the gully. Now that he knew just where the sixth man was, he cursed himself inwardly for not having realized the possibility before. The other was keeping watch along the gully, ready for any trouble like this.

He reached the next outcrop of rock, paused behind it, ears alert for the faintest sound. The small hairs on the back of his neck crawled. Every moment, he expected to feel the leaden impact of a slug tearing into his body. Then he caught the faint scrape of a heel against rock and stiffened, pressing himself tightly into the gully wall. The sound froze him once again. Stealthily, he began to edge forward again, the distant lowing of the cattle as they bawled in protest drowning out any slight sound he made, and adding to the blazing anger he felt inside him. Those were his cattle; at least, some of them were, and the others had also been stolen. Nothing mattered now, as far as he was concerned, but to destroy these men, take as many of them with him as he could. He had been in similar situations as this during those long, battle-weary days in the Wilderness, waiting for the Yankees to come driving through the dense thickets. He felt no fear now, but the familiar ways of caution came back to him. With an infinite care he placed one foot in front of the other, resting his weight on each leg before trusting it to the other. There was a noise, clambering boots on the rocks, and then silence. He tightened his lips, pressed his teeth tightly together until the muscles of his cheeks stood out under the skin, his eyes narrowed to mere slits. A wide brimmed hat came into view as he wormed his way around the out-jutting rock. The man was not taking much care about keeping his eyes open for trouble. He had his back to Ross, was leaning one shoulder against the rocky wall, his head bent forward as he struck a match, shielding the flame against the faint breeze which seemed to be funnelled along the gully. Ross waited patiently for the puff of blue smoke which told him that the other had the cigarette lit. Flipping his gun as he drew it from its holster, he held smooth barrel tightly in his right hand, fingers clasped so firmly around it that he felt the foresight biting into his flesh. His left hand reached out, closing like an iron vice over the man's mouth, jerking his head back. He felt the other struggle against him, legs threshing wildly as he tried to kick at Ross's legs with the spurs on his heels. Teeth closed on Ross's fingers as the man tried to bite into them. Then he lifted his right hand, brought the butt of the gun down with a solid thud in the very centre of the wide-brimmed hat. The man went limp instantly, sagged heavily against him. Ross held the inert weight against his arm for a moment, then lowered the other gently to the ground. There was blood on his fingers where the other had bitten deeply into them.

Breathing heavily, he drew himself upright, forced his thudding heart into a slower, more normal beat. Stepping over the uncon-scious man, he reached the sharp bend in the gully, glanced around the corner and saw to his surprise that it opened out quickly at this point, that he could see right down into the vast depression where the cattle had been herded. They were not even bothering to change the brands on these cows; they were so sure that they had the law behind them, that no one could touch them, even though they were no better than rustlers.

He felt the ire rise in his throat, threatening to choke him. There was only one way to deal with rustlers, he told himself fiercely. Gently, he eased the Colt from its holster, checked that each of the chambers was loaded, then moved forward, crouching down. The two riders were already pounding around the edge of the herd, their work of bedding it down for the afternoon virtually finished. Bending forward, Ross lined up the sights of the revolver on the leading man, squeezed the trigger. The man was rearing up in the saddle when the shot hit him squarely in the chest. The stiffness melted instantly from his bones as he slumped sideways, then fell from the saddle, his body hitting the dirt beneath the flailing hooves of his mount. His companion reined up sharply, jerking on the reins so that his mount reared in sudden fright, almost unseating him, but causing Ross to miss with his second shot. Before he could sight on the other again, the man had slid from the saddle and gone down out of sight behind his mount.

Seconds later, there was the whining scream of ricocheting slugs as they hit the rocks around him. He knew now that he had to face up to the combined fire of the remaining four men, alerted by the first two shots. A bullet hummed within an inch of his head and there was the sharp crack of a rifle shot from his right. Ducking, he shifted position rapidly, scurrying sideways among the rocks, feeling the loose shale and stones slide under his feet with every step he took.

Ross's jaw clenched. A swift glance told him that the men had moved out of cover, were swinging around to box him in against the canyon wall and then rush him. He swung his gaze behind him swiftly. If they succeeded in cutting him off from his horse, he had no chance at all. He considered moving forward, but a fusillade of bullets, spanging off the rocks close to his head told him that such a move would be fatal. There was only one thing for him to do; get back to his horse and ride out before they surrounded him.

Slugs continued to slap viciously into the rocks on either side of the him as he ducked and weaved his way along the canyon. A man yelled something harsh and loud to his right. There was a crack as blue smoke jetted from the muzzle of a rifle. He felt something scorch along his upper arm, almost released his hold on the Colt at the jarring agony of it, gritted his teeth and ran on. The rifle was hammering away again, nearer this time and out of the corner of his vision he caught fragmentary glimpses of the man running from cover to cover, striving to keep pace with him, although it was difficult to do among the boulders.

Cursing savagely, he rounded a bend, came on his mount, still standing patiently where he had left it. Slipping the reins free, he vaulted into the saddle and clung like grim death as the horse leapt forward the instant he raked spurs along its flanks. A couple of slugs hummed over his shoulder as he bent low in the saddle, the horse's hoofs kicking up a cloud of dust which temporarily hid him from view.

A moment later, he hit the river, plunged in without pausing, felt the wall of water hit the animal's chest as it struck. The water, jetting high into the air blinded him for a moment, but the yelling behind him told him that the rest of the men were hard on his heels. Through a roaring in his ears, he caught the sound of one of them shouting orders. The men now had him in their sights, were firing as they rode down to the river bank. Desperately, he kicked at his horse, forced it on. The saddle leather creaked as the water hit it. Then they were in midstream, where the current caught them. The horse began to swim, lunged forward, striking out for the further bank. Water spurted around him as bullets struck. There was a movement among the cedars along the river near a bend and he swung sharply in the saddle, sent two shots into the trees, saw a man fall forward, hit the water and go under. An arm appeared for a second above the surface, then vanished. With the water out of his eyes, he had the men pinpointed now. Three of them, two racing along the trail for the river, firing as they came. The other had swung around, was working his way rapidly through the trees, aiming for the river a short distance away, hoping to put his mount across and swing around to box Ross in.

The horse hit firm ground, snorted its relief, then clambered up on to the bank. Once among the trees, he was forced to ride more slowly and off to his right he could hear the unmistakable sound of the third man crashing his way through the brush, striving to get ahead of him. He fired twice, knew he had not hit the man, but answering shots came at him from two different directions, warning him of trouble if he hesitated.

44

He broke out of the trees two minutes later, put his mount to the upgrade. A swift glance over his shoulder told him that the others had not yet come out of the timber. Their eagerness lost them Ross Halloran. They swung too far to the right and by the time they came out of the brush, he was across the narrow stretch of open ground and spurring madly up the steep slope of the hill. Ross concentrated the whole of his riding skill into using the strength of his mount to its best advantage. There were treacherous stretches of ground on the lee of the hill and the pain in his arm, where the slug had creased the flesh was beginning to make itself felt. The horse had a good turn of speed but he had been riding for most of the day and there was tiredness in the animal which he could feel as well as sense.

They reached a flat stretch of ground, raced along it and then Ross put the horse to the final slope. Even the lightly-loaded animal was blowing hard by the time they reached the top and a swift turn in the saddle showed him that the three men were still on his trail. Even as he paused, a rifle cracked out and a rock, less than four feet from him, splintered as the bullet struck it. The distance was more than four hundred feet, he estimated, but there had been little wrong with that man's aim. He knew that there might be more rifles searching him out and swung his mount, veering in until his legs scraped the edge of the rocky cliff that rose along one side of the trail. Looking back and down, he saw that the leading rider had halted his mount, was steadying himself in the saddle to get in a more accurate shot. The bullet missed him by less than a foot, scuttling along the rocks at the trail's edge. He gigged his mount forward, put it to the steep downgrade, then paused for a moment and studied his situation, glancing about him. The winding canyon made its slow, gradual turn into more rough country some two hundred feet below him, twisting away until it came to the flat land at the bottom of the hill. Across the trail, the heavy shoulder of a ridge came down, crowding out the smaller rocks in thick folds of stone and low, stunted timber. He kicked at his horse's flanks, forced it down the slope as quickly as he dared and was halfway down, nearing the tall ridge before he heard the renewed break of gunfire at his back.

He fought his way over some of the roughest country in the area and, on occasion, he was forced to dismount and lead the horse along twisting, narrow trails which were little more than game runs. Then he was out of the hills and riding swiftly for the ranch house. The men might not, he knew, try to follow him there. They would see where he went, then report back to town. If they did decide to follow him, he felt sure that it would be possible to fight them off.

Reaching the house, he swung swiftly from the saddle on the run, let the horse halt in front of the low porch. Five minutes later, from the window overlooking the courtyard, he watched the three mounted men on top of the hill rein up their mounts and remain there for several minutes, watching the place before turning their horses and riding off out of sight.

'You got any idea who they were?' asked Faro, standing beside him. He gave Ross the benefit of his hard gaze.

'No. Only that they had some of our cattle. I knocked one out and shot two of 'em. Those are the other three.'

'They'll ride into town for the sheriff.' Mrs Halloran spoke softly from the doorway. 'I've seen it happen before. They use the law to run us off the range.'

Ross turned to face her, stared into her deep-set eyes. They were neither sad nor interested – merely empty. Resigned almost to the inevitable.

'Then I figure I'll just stay around here and wait. See what they mean to do. Seems wrong to me that the law can stop a man from defending his own home and cattle.'

'Things have changed a lot in the South since you rode away to the war, son,' said Mrs Halloran quietly. 'They don't mean to let us forget that we've been defeated. They regard us as fair spoil now.'

'You remember Chancy Vale, had the spread a couple of miles to the south,' put in Faro tightly. He turned away from his contemplation of the hilltop. 'I worked there for almost a year before I came here. There were seven of us on the payroll. When these *hombres* came and began to take off the cattle, Chancy decided he'd rather fight than see everythin' he'd worked for destroyed. We caught a bunch after they'd driven off part of the herd, wounded three and put the rest to flight. Two days later, the sheriff rode in with a posse. They hung five of the boys and shot Clancy down when he tried to resist. Me – I guess I was luckier than the others. I was ridin' the perimeter wire when it happened. I discovered what had occurred when I got back. There was no more work for me there and I was ridin' out of the territory when I rode past this ranch and your Ma offered me this job. Seems like the same thing is beginnin' all over again.'

'The war was still on then,' Ross said harshly. 'Things should be different now.' He tried to put conviction into his tone, although inwardly, he knew that he did not believe it himself. The Yankees could, and did, do these things, even now when there was supposed to be peace between North and South.

It was an hour after sundown before trouble appeared. Watching from the window, Ross sighted the cloud of dust on the upper trail that wound down from the brow of the hill. It was a big outfit, he judged, from the size of the dust cloud their horses kicked up.

Ross stretched his lips back from his teeth as he inhaled the smoke from his cigarette. Faro came over, squinted into the redness of the sunset sky. He had his eyes almost shut and a little of the red light danced in them as he said: 'Here comes trouble, Ross.' Glancing obliquely at the other, he went on: 'My advice to you is to get off the ranch, light out of here and don't stop ridin' until you're well away over the desert. These men mean big trouble. You've killed two of their men and in their eyes that's murder, and a hangin' offence.'

'They was nothin' more'n rustlers and in the country, that's the hangin' offence,' he said hotly.

'That's true, only they don't see it that way, and they have the law backin' them all the way.'

Ross wanted to say something about that, tried to frame an answer in his mind, but there was nothing. He felt confused, unsure of himself. It reminded him of times during that battle for the Wilderness when he had never known from one minute to the next where they would be, nor what might happen to them. When he had seen his companions shot dead by his side and yet had somehow escaped unharmed himself. All he could say was: 'Anyway, it's much too late to think about pullin' out now.'

'Why is it?' asked Faro pointedly. He flickered a gaze towards the party of advancing men. 'They won't be here for another ten minutes, even at the rate they're comin' now. Get out through the back way, pick up my horse, it's out there now.' Faro turned appealingly to the woman standing in the doorway. 'Tell him that it's the only way for him, Mrs Halloran. If he don't go now, he'll never make it. We can't hope to shoot it out with that bunch of men and if they get him to town, he won't last a day before they have him tried, convicted, and strung up from the nearest tree.'

Mrs Halloran came forward, put a hand on Ross's arm. 'What Faro says is the truth, son. You've got to go. I've seen this coming ever since you came back. You're impetuous, headstrong, and you won't face facts. Go straight through the rear door, get Will's horse and ride on out. Maybe it won't be long before things settle back again and you can ride home. But there's no sense in you getting yourself killed.'

'But I–' he began.

'Go,' she whispered urgently. 'It's your only chance.'

He stood wholly still as she spoke and she saw his lips stretch thin and very tight over his teeth. His eyes changed a little, subtly, opening fully on her with an expression that she could never fathom nor understand, but at that moment it was as if he did not understand what she said, nor the reason behind it.

From the window, Faro said urgently. 'Hurry, for God's sake, Ross! They're headin' down through the meadow now.'

The sound of hoofbeats grew nearer and more menacing now. Deep inside him, there was the feel of inexorable time urging him to a decision. If he stayed, as every instinct told him he should, there would be no chance. Even if they took him alive, there would be that short trial and then the shorter drop from the end of a rope thrown over a low branch. There was no justice in the South now.

'They're ridin' past the bunkhouse,' Faro said tautly. He whirled and caught Ross by the arm. 'Get goin' through the back door before they think of sending men out to surround the place. You've only got a couple of minutes before you're finished and there's nothin' you can do if you stay here except maybe sacrifice yourself for nothin'.'

Still Ross hesitated. He knew, more surely than he had ever known anything in his life before, that this was the end of a chapter for him and the beginning of something new, something unguessable that would stretch away in front of him until he came to the end of this new, fresh trail. Once he rode away from here he would be a wanted man, an outlaw; because those men out there would not stop until they had hunted him down. Even this wide territory would not be big enough to hold him. Once, out in the Wilderness, he had felt like this; when a large force of the Union men had surrounded the small group which he had commanded. There had been no other course open to him but to order the men to disperse and try to work their way back through the enemy lines, to regroup once they were clear. It had been an order he had hated giving. Every instinct then had been to stand and fight, to take as many of the enemy with him as he could before the end came.

'You in there,' roared a voice from the dimness outside. 'This is Sheriff Lawrence. I've got a warrant here for the arrest of Ross Halloran on a charge of murder. Are you comin' out quietly or do we have to come in and take you?'

'Please, Ross.' His mother came forward, pulled him reluctantly towards the far door. 'Take Will's horse and ride out of here. Get as far away as you can. Maybe, in a little while, things will be different and you can come back and take over the ranch as your father would have liked.'

'And if those men out there aren't content to take a handful of cattle every now and again. If they decide to take the ranch and everythin' on it?'

'Then that's God's will,' she said simply. 'At the moment, all I care about is that you get away from here before they take you, dead or alive.'

'All right.' He nodded his head tersely. 'I'll go. But I promise you, that these men will regret this.' Instinct forced Ross to move forward. Behind him, he heard another shout. Then he was through the door at the back of the ranch, out on the rear porch. The horse was there, standing patiently as Will had told him, tethered to the small hitching rail. He threw a swift look in both directions, then leapt on the back of the animal, and urged it out.

3

Vengeance Rider

Three days later, south and west of the ranch, Ross found that his trail led him through a brown-earthed, vast depression where rocky gulches and dense chaparral thickets made the trail twist and wind like a snake's belly, cutting through some of the worst country that he had ever known. Shortly after midday, he reined up in a small hollow, where a wide, rocky overhang provided a little shade from the direct, scorching rays of the sun. There were few other shadows and he knew that he would find no better place for some miles. Dismounting, he settled his shoulders back against the sunheated rock and rested his weary body. The long days in the saddle had worn his limbs raw and all the time he had been riding, the hate had been building up inside him, the slow-burning anger that was like a white-hot flame, becoming more and more difficult for him really to control.

Like his father, he had been tolerant and generally easygoing, but he was also acutely conscious that he had inherited the other's ferocious temper; but in him it did not flare out uncontrollably, rather it tended to smoulder away, unnoticed by others, beneath the surface. Before the war had come, he had encountered few really malicious characters and any man he had fought had not held it against him when the fight had ended. But now, these men from the North, men he had fought with honour on the field of battle, were moving in and taking everything they could lay their hands on. He remembered with anger and loathing, those men he had seen riding off with the cattle, the sheriff who had ridden out of town, enforcing these laws made up to protect the Northern robbers against the people of the South who only wished to forget the dreadful war and settle down to the task of rebuilding the country into something worthwhile again.

He built himself a smoke, lit it and dragged the smoke down into his lungs. His mouth felt parched and dry, his lips cracked, and he gained very little satisfaction and refreshment from the cigarette. He was not sure about this stretch of country, had never ridden this way before; and there was no telling when he would next find water in this hell hole of a desert. His canteen was a little less than half full at the moment, he reckoned, shaking it. Better to try not to drink any more than he could help.

Shifting his head back a little, he squinted up at the heavens, where he could just glimpse the molten globe of the sun, now at the peak of its slow climb. Soon it would begin to dip down to the western horizon, but there would be no let-up from the heat until an hour or so before sundown. The worst of the day was yet to come and in this wasteland, the heat would be intolerable.

As he had ridden, he had kept his gaze switching from one side to the other, had guessed that this was about the narrowest part of the Badlands which stretched perhaps fifty or a hundred miles in one direction, maybe twenty or so in the other. The river he had forded shortly after pulling away from the ranch bordered one edge of the desert and there would undoubtedly be another on the far side; but in between there might be no waterholes at all; although some of the old-timers spoke of hidden wells which could be found if one knew where to start digging for them.

The trouble was that there was no one, apart from a few outlaws like himself, and roving bands of Indians, keeping away from the white man, who cared to explore the Badlands. The stage route moved well to the north, through the thick timber which was, however, much to be preferred to this trail. Shortly after riding into the desert he had discovered the reason why Wells Fargo had chosen to add so many miles to their route.

Finishing his smoke, he whistled up his mount, climbed back into the saddle and continued westward. He did not press his horse, but the animal was a good one and they made excellent progress in spite of the rough terrain. He recalled what little he knew of this part of the territory. On the far side of the desert he would cross the river and then enter more amenable country before coming to the township of Clarkson. This was still a lawless frontier where for most men the life was hard and only the strong and the ruthless survived. To the south, still bordering the Badlands, rose the high peaks of the Snake Mountains, a barrier that lay stretched across the horizon. Wild and mostly inaccessible, they were sparsely inhabited, with only a few outlaws residing there, men who deliberately shunned the main trails.

The sun was almost down when he reached the river, but some hours of clear daylight still remained. Alighting, he loosened the cinch and then went forward, going down on his knees, washing the dust from his face and neck. After drinking his fill, he sat on a large rock, ate a little of the dried meat and washed it down with the clear, cold water from the river.

He was on the point of lighting the cigarette he had just rolled when a sudden sound jerked him around, his hand dropping to the gun at his waist. Then he froze as two men stepped out of the low trees, moving around to come on him from the side. Both were bearded and unkempt, one carrying a rifle in his hands with the barrel pointed at Ross's stomach. The other man, taller, with a wolfish sharpness to his face, made no attempt to pull his gun, but came up to where Ross sat and said thinly: 'I wouldn't reach for that Colt if I was you, mister. There are two rifles trained on you from the bushes yonder, apart from the one that Blade is carryin'.'

Bright blue eyes regarded Ross sharply from beneath bushy eyebrows. He hooked his thumbs into the sagging leather belt around his middle.

Ross knew himself to be in great danger as two more men came shuffling out of the bushes, their Sharps rifles trained on him. These looked like outlaws from the Badlands. 'Just what is this?' he asked harshly. 'A hold-up? If it is, you'll get little from me.'

'At the moment we're just curious,' said the tall man. 'Ain't often that anybody tries ridin' through the Badlands alone. Not unless he's a lawman trailin' somebody, or somebody on the run like us.' He scrutinized Ross keenly.

Sitting, apparently at ease, in the midst of these men, Ross told them quietly of the happenings which had forced him to run, the manner in which he had killed two men and what was likely to happen if he was caught.

Blade eyed him closely for a moment, then lowered the rifle a little. 'Durned if I don't believe him, Hank.' he said, turning to the tall man.

'Just what were you figurin' on doin' out here?' asked the man called Hank, still evidently suspicious.

'I haven't got that rightly figured out,' Ross said quietly. 'Anythin' that might even the score a little will be all right by me.'

Hank rubbed a hand over his chin, the stubble on the sunburned skin scraping harshly under his fingers. 'You say that you fought with the Confederate Army, Halloran. You know any of the men who rode with Quantrill?'

'Never met any,' Ross affirmed.

'I rode with him,' said the other thinly. His gaze was defiant as though expecting some retort from Ross. But the other merely shrugged.

'So?' he said.

Hank was silent for a moment, his glance

speculative. 'There are some who say we were nothin' more'n thieves and murderers. You got that opinion?'

'No.' Ross shook his head. 'After what happened to my place, the way these Northerners are runnin' off with the best cattle, refusin' to allow us to get stores, moving in on the land and takin' it from those who owned it rightfully before the war, I feel that way myself.'

'Good.' The other nodded. 'That's what I wanted to hear.' He stepped forward and extended his hand. 'You look like a man who knows how to handle a gun and can fight his way out of trouble.'

'I've had some experience of that,' Ross nodded. He gripped the proffered hand. He knew that many a man in the outlaw's position might have shot first and argued the identity of his victim later. He could guess that in many cases these men had been forced into this sort of life in the same way that he had; but it was plain that these could be deadly and dangerous men.

'Things have changed a lot around here,' said Blade. He lowered himself on to the smooth rock a couple of feet from Ross. 'We lost a war and none of us likes that except for the Yankee carpetbaggers who've moved

61

in and are takin' over everythin' that was once ours. We've decided that we won't just stand by and see it happen. We're goin' to take everything we can lay our hands on and if we have to use these guns to do it, then we can always tell ourselves that they brought it on their own heads.'

'How long do you figure it will be before they come in force to hunt you down?'

'They don't know this country,' averred the other confidently. 'The railroad runs fifteen miles north of here. We can hold up the bullion coaches and get our hands on that gold they're carryin'. Most of it has been taken from the South, anyway, so we're only takin' what's rightly ours.'

'Don't they have guards ridin' with these trains?' Ross asked. He watched as the other two men, having laid their rifles down on the rocks, busied themselves with lighting a fire. Clearly they knew their way around this part of the territory, knew that it was safe.

'Sure they do,' put in Hank. His lips split in a wide grin. 'But there are also the banks in Clarkson and Fort Carstairs. They're gettin' to be big places now, growin' fast.'

Ross thought the idea over and found that it appealed to him. It was one way of evening the score against the North, he reflected.

The anger which he had felt when he had ridden from the ranch, running out the back way like a scared rabbit, still hurt inside him, still rankled. He wanted to kill, to destroy.

'You take any of the banks yet?' he asked, sucking smoke down into his lungs. With the fire going, the men brought up their horses which had been hidden in the brush some distance away.

Hank coloured a little. 'Only one – why?'

'Just wonderin' how you found it.'

'There was no trouble.' His mouth twisted contemptuously. 'They sent a posse out after us, but the guerillas scouted all of this country during the last year or so of the war. We know it better than they do. They never had a chance in hell of pickin' up our trail. We're safe here until Kingdom Come, believe me.'

'But how much did you get from holdin' up the bank?'

'Two – three thousand dollars.'

'That wouldn't go far, split four ways.'

'We'll do better the next time,' Hank grunted. He motioned towards the fire, where steaks were being fried and there was hot coffee in the pot over the flames. 'Help yourself. You look as though you could do with some food and coffee in your belly.'

Two days later, the five men rode into Fort Carstairs. It was early morning, with only a faint grey light showing in the eastern sky, highlighting a few details, but with long shadows hiding most of the town. They reined up half a mile from the outskirts, on a low ridge of ground that overlooked the main freight trail through. Hank Morelle plucked the stub of the cigarette from between his lips and tossed it on to the hard ground where it winked briefly, redly, and then went out.

'We'll separate here,' he said hoarsely. 'Clem and Dane will circle around and come in from the north. Ross – you take up your position across from the bank, keep your eyes open in case of trouble and see that the horses are ready. Blade and me will go in and hold up the place. Is that all understood?'

Ross nodded with the others. He was a little uneasy about the way in which Morelle had planned the attack, but knew better than to try to force his own opinions on these men. He flexed his shoulders, took out the Colts from their holsters and checked the chambers before thrusting them back into leather again.

Hank looked straight at Clem and Dane. 'All right. Ride on out,' he ordered. 'We'll wait until you're out of sight, then ride in slow and easy. I reckon the town should come alive in half an hour or so.'

The two men gigged their mounts, wheeled them sharply away from the trail, and rode off into the growing light of dawn. Hank grinned maliciously, turned to Ross. 'Sure you know exactly what to do? Once we get the money, we head back this way, then split up and meet back at the place where we first met. Think you can find your way back there?'

'With my share of the money waitin', I'll be there,' Ross said tightly.

Morelle nodded. There was no expression on his face as he said: 'This is goin' to be the first of many, Halloran. Your share will be waitin' for you when you get there, believe me.'

Ross said nothing. Inwardly, he had the feeling that he could trust the other, that now they were bound together by a bond which was, if anything, even stronger and more permanent than that which had tied him to the rest of the men in his troop during the war. They had placed themselves outside the law and once they rode into this town and held up that bank, they would have taken an irrevocable step which would set their feet on the trail that could have only one end. No matter what anybody said, an outlaw never lived to enjoy the money he stole. There were, indeed, some who were in the game not for the money, but for the excitement, or for a sense of revenge. He smiled a little, to himself in the dimness of the early dawn as he waited for Morelle to give the word to move out. Which of these reasons applied to him? he wondered tensely. At that moment, he found it difficult to tell.

There was a long, bright streak of grey lying along the eastern horizon when Morelle tossed away his second cigarette butt, nodded briefly, then made a quick motion with his left hand. They put their horses to the downgrade, rode slowly and easily towards Fort Carstairs. In the pale grey light, Ross saw that even at this early hour there were some men abroad. A couple of bewhiskered men were seated on a wooden bench that had been erected around the base of a huge cottonwood tree which grew in the middle of the square where two main trail routes met. Hank gave them a swift glance which merely brushed over them, aware of their presence there, but anticipating no trouble from them.

As they rode into the square, Hank leaned sideways in the saddle, said in a soft tone: 'All right, Ross. Ride on down that street yonder, then swing around and come back from the other side of town. Better stake yourself out on the boardwalk yonder, where you can keep an eye on the bank and the sheriff's office.'

Ross gave an almost imperceptible nod, swung his horse and moved down the side street. He rode past the Overland Freighting Yard, with the name emblazoned in tall, garishly-painted letters over the wide gateway, on past two smaller offices, then a saloon and a hotel, situated next to each other, the latter a tall, three-storeyed building with two wide terraces running around the outside.

There was a short, thick-set man standing with his back against the wooden upright outside the freighting yard, a pipe clenched between his teeth. He surveyed Ross closely with a sharp-eyed scrutiny as he rode by, followed him with a keen attention. As he reached the end of the street where it led out into the low hills, across a dusty stretch of plain, Ross swung his mount sharply to the left, into one of the narrow, evil-smelling alleys that ran around the circumference of the town. A swift glance told him that the man at the freighting yard was still watching him, still curious. He felt a faint sense of apprehension run through him, then thrust it away. Maybe the other was only surprised to see a stranger riding into town at that time of the day. Most men timed their arrivals in town at evening, when the heat of the day was over, not caring to ride through this outlaw-infested country after dark.

As he rode, he felt the grim silence clinging around him. Inwardly, he was not sure how far he could trust Hank Morelle's plans and judgment. The fact that the others had succeeded in robbing one bank and getting away with it, meant little. He did not slacken off until he had swung around half the perimeter of the town and saw, ahead of him, the main road running right through. He gave a quick skyward glance, saw that the tops of the hills far to the west were now touched with the first red flush of sunlight. Even though the valley itself was still in the grey light of dawn, it wanted only ten or fifteen minutes for full daylight to break over the town.

He walked his mount to the spot where the narrow alley intersected the main street, paused there, making himself a smoke. Turning his head this way and that, he surveyed the scene in front of him. Some three hundred yards away, he could just make out the tall cottonwood and the two tiny figures still seated beneath it. A lone rider came into town from the far end of the street, moving his mount at a tired, jaded pace. As he approached the square, the other straightened up, and even from that distance, Ross was able to make out the faint glint of light reflected from the star the other wore on his shirt. He twisted his lips back in a derisive grin. Evidently, the sheriff had been out all night. That made things even better as far as they were concerned. A tired man was slower in his reflex actions than one who had just had a good night's sleep. The sheriff reined up in front of the office, slid from the saddle and looped the reins over the hitching rail. Then he stumped up on to the boardwalk, hesitated for a moment and looked about him, stretched himself, arms above his head, before unlocking the door and stepping inside. The door closed behind him, and the silence came back to the street, with only the hipshot horse in front of the office to indicate that anybody had come into town. Then Ross lifted his gaze and saw Hank and Blade moving forward out of one of the side alleys where they had moved so as not to be seen by the lawman. They walked their mounts to the side of the street opposite the bank building, got down and moved up on to the boardwalk where they seated themselves in the high-backed chairs, stretching out their legs in front of them, their hats pulled well down over their eyes.

In spite of the tension, Ross grinned to himself as he struck a match and lit the cigarette. To all intents and purposes, the other two were only tired men, getting a breath of air before the sun came up and the heat and dust became unbearable. He dug into his pocket, brought out the big watch which his father had given him the day he had ridden away to the war. It was a few minutes after eight o'clock. Thrusting it back into his pocket, he puffed slowly on the cigarette, drawing the sweet smoke down into his lungs. There was no sign of Clem and Dane, but he knew they would be somewhere around, staying out of sight until the time came to converge on the bank. They had worked out everything to the last minute the previous night when they had talked it over and laid their plans.

Maybe all of their carefully planned intentions would go wrong, would blow up in their faces because of some little thing which they had overlooked or could not possibly have foreseen, and then they would have to fight their way out of the town. But he knew that the men in the band were not the sort to be thrown by a bad roll of the dice.

The minutes dragged by. Ross leaned forward in the saddle, resting his arms on the pommel. The wash of sunlight moved like a river down the slopes of the distant hills, swept over the valley floor and then reached the town, flooding down the street and touching the houses and buildings with its hard, harsh glare, taking away the softer contours which had been there during the brief dawn and replacing them by the strict, functional outlines of the town, making it seem dirtier, meaner and unlovely.

Ross checked his watch once more. It was almost time. He could feel the touch of heat on his face and neck as the sun lifted higher in the east, a glaring red disc which would soon become yellow and then a fierce white as it rose towards its zenith.

There were more townsfolk about now and Ross watched them more closely, switching his gaze at intervals along the street, waiting for Morelle to give the signal. He could feel the tension beginning to mount, an electric tautness which seemed to crackle on the faint breeze that whispered along the street, just stirring the dust.

On the boardwalk, Hank and Blade had risen to their feet, were stepping down into the street. He clearly saw Blade hitch his gunbelt a little higher around his middle as they made their way across to the bank.

Touching spurs to his mount's flanks, he walked the horse slowly along the middle of the street, keeping his gaze unfocused, watching everyone on either side of him, not seeing their faces, merely aware of them as he rode by. Hank and Blade had paused just outside the bank as he drew level with the building. Less than half a minute later, Clem and Dane rode around the corner twenty yards away.

Edging his horse to the other side of the street, Ross slid from the saddle, making every movement nonchalant and unobtrusive. Looping the reins slackly over the rail next to Hank's mount, with Blade's next to it, he walked on to the boardwalk, for the moment taking no notice of anything that was going on behind him on the other side of the street. When he had seated himself, he looked across at the bank. Hank and Blade were already inside, and Clem and Dane had moved forward, were on the point of entering. He forced himself to relax, leaning back in the wicker chair, legs thrust out straight in front of him, arms placed loosely to front of him, his hands in his lap. Only a keen-eyed observer would have seen that his fingers were less than two inches from the butts of the guns in his belt, that his legs, seeming lax, were actually braced and ready to heave him to his feet at a moment's notice.

He slitted his eyes against the flooding sunlight and concentrated all his gaze on the door of the bank in front of him, only occasionally switching his glance towards the sheriff's office further along the street. Still no sign of trouble. He began to breathe a little easier. If everything was going according to plan, the men would have covered all of the people in the bank by now, employees and customers and the money would be scooped into the carefully folded wheat sacks which they had carried inside under their arms.

Five minutes passed. In spite of the silence, Ross could feel the muscles of his chest and stomach churning painfully into hard knots. He was acutely aware that there was sweat on the palms of his hands and he wiped them on the cloth of his pants. A door opened down the street. He glanced swiftly sideways, saw the sheriff come out of the building, stand on the boardwalk just in front of the door, knuckling his fists into his eyes. Ross brushed the tips of the fingers of his right hand over the smooth butt of the gun. Gently, he eased himself to his feet. The sheriff showed no sign of coming in their direction, seemed to be merely contemplating the street scene.

If the lawman made a move towards the bank and there was any trouble inside the building, Ross knew he would first have to shoot down the sheriff and then take care of anyone else on the street.

He sucked in a gust of air, moved to the edge of the rail, stood with his feet on the edge of the boardwalk watching every movement of the lawman. The other had turned his head away, was squinting up at the sun as though trying to guess what kind of a day it was going to turn out to be. There was a deep stillness lying over the town, a heavy, almost oppressive silence that rang in Ross's ears as he waited.

Then, with a shocking abruptness, there came the roar of a gunshot from inside the bank. At the same instant, the doors were flung open and the four men came piling out into the street, three of them clutching the wheat sacks, bulging with loot, the fourth, Dane, backing them up, turning and firing into the open doorway.

Ross leapt forward, saw Clem and Dane run along the street a little way to where their mounts were tethered. He dropped down into the dust, caught at the reins of his own mount and also unloosened those for Hank and Blade as the two men came darting forward across the street. Out of the corner of his eye, Ross saw the sheriff swing round sharply, his hand dropping to the gun at his waist as he let out a loud cry of warning and sprinted forward. The fact that he had probably been riding hard all night did not appear to have impaired his reflexes as much as Ross had thought. A shot rang out and the bullet chipped a slice of wood from the upright just behind him, sending it skimming over his shoulder.

The men and women in the street scattered as more shots rang out. Dane and

Clem were firing now, backing up the other three. Swiftly, without hesitation, Ross swung himself up into the saddle, jerked on the reins, pulling his horse's head around, kicking vigorously at its flanks with the spurs. It leapt forward as though suddenly unleashed, catching up with the others in a few strides, racing along the dusty street. More shots rang out from behind them and he saw Clem jerk in the saddle, sway, then somehow, maintain his grip on the reins, clinging desperately with his knees as his mount reared. Turning, Ross jerked his own gun out, fired swiftly behind him. He saw the sheriff, running into the middle of the street, suddenly crumple, double in the middle as the slug hit him in the stomach. The gun dropped from his nerveless fingers and he toppled forward on to his face to lie still in the dirt.

A few desultory shots followed them from the middle of the town. One of the bank employees had appeared in the open doorway of the building, a shotgun clutched in his hands. He sighted and fired swiftly, but most of that terrible rain of fire went wild. Something unseen, plucked at Ross's sleeve as he bent low over the neck of his mount, flattening himself as much as possible on its back to present a more difficult target.

But although they had left most of the opposition behind near the square in the middle of the town, there was still a gauntlet of fire to be run. The sound of the shots and the commotion had been heard all the way along the street and as they drew level with a couple of stores, one of which Ross noticed was a gunsmiths, three men burst out on to the narrow boardwalk, clutching weapons in their hands, aiming them and firing at the outlaws as they raced past, with no thought for themselves. In the heat of the moment, they had clearly overlooked the fact that they were exposing themselves to return fire. Hank fired several shots at them. Most of the slugs went wild, smashing in the windows, sending shards of glass cascading into the street. One of the men, a burly, black-faced man, clutched at his stomach, reeled backward and then sat down as though suddenly tired of everything. A scattergun roared from the dim shadows of the boardwalk and the hail of lead lashed through the air immediately behind the five men as they rode by without slackening their speed.

Now the end of the street was in sight.

Clem was rolling in the saddle like a drunken man, his face white, beaded with sweat. He kept running his tongue over his lips as he struggled to force the pain and weakness away, to keep himself in the saddle, knowing that once he fell, there would be no chance for him, that none of his companions would halt and get him back on to his horse. There would be too much at stake for that.

Somehow, he made it, sweat streaking his face, running down his cheeks, mixing with the dust mask from which only his eyes peered out, the only part of his features which seemed to be alive. The bullet had hit him in the back, in the middle of his left shoulder, burning its way down to the bone. A red wall of agony fogged his vision and there was a dull roaring in his ears which would not go away. He could feel the weakness seeping through his arms and legs, and his whole body seemed to be going numb. There was the warm, sticky feeling of blood oozing from the wound and soaking into his shirt and every movement of his mount made the pain worse, jarring redly into his body until he seemed to exist inside a swelling balloon of agony which, once it burst, would send him straight to death.

He forced his eyes to stay open, pushing his sight through the wavering red haze, straining to make out the end of the road that led out of Fort Carstairs. Once they got away from the town and out into that rocky country which lay to the south-west, there might be a chance to rest up somewhere and get this lead out of him. For he knew, with a sudden sick certainty, that unless they did, he would not live.

4

Badlands Renegades

They rode at a swift run through the narrow cut of a dry creek, sheltered from sight by the high banks that rose steeply on either side of them. Now that they were well away from the town and appeared to have thrown off any initial pursuit, Ross began to feel a little of the heightened anticipation. As they came out of the creek, he threw a swift glance behind him, narrowed his eyes against the vicious sunglare and knew that his anticipation had been premature. There was a faint dust cloud on their trail, perhaps a mile away, but it told him as it did the others, that a posse had been formed quickly in town, in spite of the death of the sheriff, and there were armed men on their trail.

Evidently Morelle had the same trapped feeling, for he reined up, said harshly. 'All right, we split up here like we planned. Scatter and we'll meet out near the Badlands.'

There was nothing more said. The men knew better than to argue. Ross threw a swift glance at Clem where he lolled awkwardly in the saddle, saw Dane move over to the other. Then he had swung away from them, was spurring his mount away from the narrow creek, out over the stretching plain, filled with the mesquite and a few stunted bushes, but with a heavy line of timber about a mile distant where he might be able to throw off any pursuit if they decided to follow him.

He rode his horse up the slope a few minutes later into the tall cedars at the top. He saw then that the brush grew heavier in front of him interspersed with rocks and on the far side of the long ledge the country was rougher, cut here and there by rocky upthrusts that made any trail a twisting, winding thing, difficult to follow. It was impossible to hurry a horse through this kind of terrain. It needed only one wrong step and the animal's leg would be snapped cleanly in two like a rotten twig. Except for a rustling rise of quail as he rode through the timber and a sudden streaking flight of longhorn that darted through the brush, there was no sign of life as he headed north and the country lay still and silent and apparently lifeless on every side of him.

Once, he paused and swung himself in the saddle, straining his ears to pick out the sound of any pursuit. He caught a far-off echo, but it was not repeated and although he listened for a full minute, there was no further sound and he pushed on, more relaxed. It was likely that the posse had seen him break away from the others, but had decided to follow the larger group. Guiding the horse skilfully down the slope, he reached the stretch of country beyond the rocky gullies and ridge. Here and there, he rode over smooth lava flows where the molten magma from the deep core of the earth had spewed up to the surface in some long-past age, had cooled and now lay spread over the ground in dark, grey-purple sheets, ringing with a curiously metallic sound as his horse moved over them.

An hour later, with the sun lifting towards its zenith and the heat lying heavy and oppressive over the country, he reined up where a small creek splashed over a smooth, stony bed and let his horse blow for a while. Kneeling, he scooped up the water in the palm of his hand, drinking thirstily, rubbing some of the white dust from his face where it had formed a thick mask. Sitting back on his haunches, he contemplated his position. Another two hours ought to bring him to the rendezvous. Once he got near to the spot, however, it would be well if he rode carefully, keeping his eyes and ears open. He had taken a roundabout route and the others ought to have got there before him. But if the posse had kept on their trail, they might be waiting to jump him.

Rolling himself a cigarette, he thrust the brown-paper cylinder between his lips and lit it, drawing the smoke down into his lungs. He gained little pleasure from the cigarette, but it gave him the chance to think things over in his mind. Just where did he go from here once he had been given his share of the loot from the bank? he wondered. Did he stay with these men, live the life of an outlaw, or did he ride on, taking the money with him and head for the border, staying one jump ahead of the law?

The low boughs of a cedar scraped and rustled suddenly at his back. Ross froze at the sound, heard the faint snicker of a horse among the timber, guessed instantly that he had been fooling himself all the time, that someone had been trailing him and had kept out of sight, concealing himself cleverly in the undergrowth. He twisted his head, jumped to one side in the same movement, just as a gun lashed at him from the bushes. The bullet hit the dirt within a foot of his prone body. Swiftly, he rolled over and over, dragging the Colt from his holster, thumbing back the hammer as he came up on one knee, pushing his sight into the tangled greenness of the undergrowth, searching for any sign of movement that would give away the position of the attacker. The nearest cover was a piece of deadwood some ten yards away and he cast about him anxiously trying to decide whether he had a chance at all of making it before the other fired again.

Then, at the corner of his vision, he spotted the faint drifting cloud of blue gunsmoke. In the still air it hovered over the bush immediately beneath one of the cedars. Without hesitation, he fired a couple of shots, one on either side of the spot, then a third dead centre. There was a faintly audible grunt, followed by the sound of a heavy body collapsing against the twigs. Jerking himself to his feet, he thrust himself forward over the loose soil, diving for the cover of the log. Flinging himself bodily over it, he lay gasping, dragging air into his lungs, squirming around to face the bush. Another shot came from the man behind the cedar and a chip of wood flew from the top of the log, skimming over Ross's shoulder. He ducked swiftly, thumbed fresh shells into the empty chambers of his gun. Wounded or not, there had been nothing wrong with the other's aim.

'All right, mister. You come on out,' called a sudden, rasping voice. 'If you ain't out here with your hands lifted when I count ten, we'll kill you.'

Ross froze. That voice had come from a spot more than ten yards from where he knew the other man to be hidden. So there were at least two of them. He cursed himself for not having thought of this before. He had been a goddamned fool, riding in here and stopping to drink without taking the proper precautions. He was an ex-Army man. He ought to have known better than to rest up without scouting the area first, particularly since he had known that there was a posse after their band.

He lowered his head still further, listening for any furtive movements in the brush. There was, of course, just the chance that the posse had split up to follow them all, and only two of them, at the most three, had ridden after him, the others following Morelle and the rest of the men. If he could only be sure how many men there were, he could perhaps find a way out of this mess. Once he gave himself up, he was finished. A quick, trial, if any, and then the short, swift, kicking end with a rope around his neck.

Wriggling to the end of the log, he gently moved his head to squint around the deadfall, aimed at the spot where he reckoned the second gunman to be, and squeezed off three shots, the roar merging into one sudden explosion.

Pandemonium broke loose almost at once. He heard someone yell an order in a harsh voice, then more gunshots rang out. Crouching low, he counted them, knowing that every man who opposed him would be firing. A few moments later, he felt a vague relief. There were three men out there and he felt sure that he had wounded one of them, perhaps badly.

As he lay in the soft earth, protected by the huge bulk of the deadfall, he visualized the position in his mind's eye. There was at least ten yards of open ground between him and the nearest point of the timber and undergrowth. None of the three men could move in on him and take him by surprise. But by the same token, he was pinned down, unable to move without exposing himself to their fire.

Ross edged himself into position, braced his legs against the ground. There was a smouldering look in his eyes as he inched his head upward to get a glimpse of the line of undergrowth that grew rampantly along the edge of the cedars. He took slow, deep breaths of air before glancing over the rim of the log, the Colt gripped tightly in his fist, his finger bar-straight on the trigger, ready to fire at the slightest movement in the brush. There was the faint jingle of a harness from somewhere close by and he knew instinctively that it was not from his own mount. He switched his gaze, saw the two horses standing patiently just inside the rim of bushes. Their reins were wedged into a cleft in the branches of one of the trees and both animals were definitely uneasy. There was another shot from the underbrush.

Oblivious to his own precarious position, he pulled himself forward, bracing his legs under him. He caught a glimpse of the face a split second before the man saw him. The gun in his hand barked once and he saw the man reel back as the slug took him cleanly between the eyes. The man crashed back and lay still. For a moment there was silence, then the same voice that he had heard before yelled: 'This is the law here, mister. You can't hope to buck the whole state. Give yourself up now and I'll personally see to it that you get a fair trial.'

Like hell you will, thought Ross bitterly. He loosed off a couple of shots in the direction of the other's voice, but the man must have guessed his intention and had shifted his position before Ross fired. There was the shrill whine of ricocheting slugs glancing off rocks and splintering the wooden log behind which he crouched. He had certainly lessened the odds. Now there were only the two facing him and he felt sure that one of them had been hit by his first shots.

Ross pressed his lips tightly together, tried to figure out where the third man was, the man he had hit. He did not doubt that the only reason this man kept calling out to him, giving his position away, was to draw all of Ross's attention to him, leaving that other man free to skirt around him, take him from an unexpected direction. He managed a grim smile as he heard the faint, but unmistakable sound of breaking twigs off to his left. So that was it. The wounded man was making heavy progress striving to move without making any sound and giving himself away. But it had been his inability to move quietly because of his wound, that had betrayed him.

Narrowing his eyes, Ross kept his gaze fixed on a narrow opening among the trees. He guessed that the other would have to work his way across it within a few moments if he continued along the way he was now moving. Sure enough, less than fifteen seconds later, the humped shape of the lawman showed as he began to worm his way forward. This was not the time for any niceties, for doing the honourable thing of calling the other out. He flexed the muscles of his arm and shoulder where they had become cramped from remaining in the same position for so long, then drew a careful bead on the other and squeezed the trigger. The gun jerked against his wrist with the recoil and he saw the man jerk, then lie quite still. There was no further movement out of him and Ross knew that he was dead. A wounded man would not have remained there in the open where he could be picked off by the next bullet, but would have forced himself under cover as quickly as possible.

'Now there are just the two of us,' Ross called tersely. 'You want to step out and finish this man to man?'

There was no reply from the man in the brush. Ross waited tensely. A few moments later, there was the sound of a horse being spurred away, deep in the trees. He paused for a further moment, then took a gamble and got slowly to his feet. No bullet came from the trees. The last man had decided that discretion was the better part of valour and had ridden off rather than shoot it out with him on even terms. Ross's lips curled in a derisive grin. Thrusting the Colt back into its holster, he walked back to his horse.

Leaving the bodies of the two dead deputies in the brush, he rode out and swung south again, reaching the main trail ninety minutes later. He soon picked up the marks of horses, noticed one set of tracks with a split shoe that he knew belonged to Blade's horse. The other men must have joined up here and then ridden on to the meeting place together. There was no sign that they had been found by the rest of the posse. A swift glance to the north told him that the trail was empty as far as the eye could see.

He reached the rendezvous half an hour later. The four men were seated in the shadow of the tall overhang, their horses grazing near the stream. Morelle glanced up as he rode in, his hand came to the butt of his gun. He relaxed visibly as he saw who it was, let his hand fall loosely by side.

'Thought that the posse had caught up with you, Halloran,' he said softly. His gaze never once left Ross's face. 'We saw a bunch of 'em swing around after you.'

Ross slid wearily from the saddle. There was a fire burning on the flat rock, most of the smoke caught and trapped beneath the overhanging so that it would not be seen from a distance. Letting his mount move over to the others, he squatted by the fire.

'Three of them jumped me a while back,' he said harshly. 'I had to kill two of 'em. The third decided he'd had enough and ran out.'

'You see anythin' of the rest of the posse on the way here?' asked Blade. He held a piece of cooked meat on the tip of his knife for a moment and then tipped it down his throat.

'No sign at all. Reckon they must've given up the chase.'

'Could be,' grunted Morelle, non-committally. 'But with that sheriff shot dead, it ain't likely. This place is goin' to become unhealthy for us in a little while. I figure we should divide the money and split up. Ride on out of here.'

'Why split up?' Ross asked, switching his gaze from one man to the other. 'Seems to me that we make a good team. There's rich pickings to be had in this territory for anybody who's willing to take a few risks for 'em.'

Morelle drew his black brows together into a straight line, stared intently at Ross. 'Just what have you got in mind?' he asked thinly.

Ross shrugged. 'Why stop at hittin' the banks? The big money isn't there, it's on the stages or the trains.'

Morelle stared at him for a moment, then scratched his chin. 'I don't like the idea of tryin' to hold up the trains,' he said finally. 'They have too many guards ridin' on them. Besides, take money from the railroad and we'll have the Pinkerton men on our necks. Them and the railroad detectives. At least with the banks, we only have to outrun the local posse. If we followed your plan, we'd have the entire territory after us. Pretty soon, there'd be no place for us to run.'

'You scared of them?' Ross asked. There was a faint insult in his tone.

Morelle dropped his hand quickly, impulsively, to the gun at his waist, eyes narrowed angrily. For a moment, his tongue licked along his dry lips. Then, with an effort, he relaxed.

'Don't tempt me to shoot you, Halloran,' he said softly. 'I'm scared of nobody, but I like to think I'll live to spend the money I get. There's a nice little place over the border in Mexico that I've had my eye on ever since the war finished. I mean to go there and settle down, live the life of a gentleman. If I was to fall in with your plans, I'd be dead within six months. You have to be big and good to fight the railroad.'

Ross eyed him intently for a moment, then flicked a look at Blade. 'What about you?' he asked tautly. 'You think the same way as Hank?'

Blade stared at him for a long moment in silence, then shrugged his shoulders. 'You reckon that there's a chance we could get away with it?' he asked, trying to disguise the eagerness in his voice.

'A good chance,' Ross said. 'Everythin' would have to be planned, down to the last detail. But so long as nobody knows what we look like, we could ride into town and masquerade as business men, get to know what the trains are carrying when they'll be passing through the stations along the route.'

'You're talking mighty big for somebody who's just been in on his first hold-up,' said Morelle. He made to say something more, but a moan from Clem interrupted him.

The other was lying with his back and shoulders against the rock, his face ashen, the mask of dust making his complexion seem even more pallid. There was blood on the back of his shirt and whenever he coughed, a little of it flecked his lips and dribbled down his chin.

'You've got to get me to a doctor, Hank.' he said hoarsely, jerking the words out through shaking lips. 'This slug has to come out.'

'Don't talk like a fool,' snapped the other. 'You know damned well there ain't a thing we can do yet. Maybe after it's dark we'll take you into Clarkson. We can't go back to Fort Carstairs.'

'It'll be too late then. I'm losin' too much

blood. Damnit!' The other's voice thinned and lifted to a shout. Sweat stood out on his forehead, glistened in the light. 'Are you goin' to keep me here until I'm dead?' He paused for a moment, let that thought sink into his mind, then lifted his head sharply as a fresh thought struck him. 'That's it, isn't it, Morelle? You mean to let me die so that you have only the four-way split. It means more for you, doesn't it?'

'Keep quiet and stop babbling like a madman,' snapped Morelle harshly. 'We've been forced to listen to you ever since we got back. I keep tellin' you that we'll get you to a doctor as soon as we can, but I don't intend puttin' my neck in a noose just for you. Now keep quiet!'

Clem relapsed into a sullen silence, his face twisted in pain. Ross waited for a moment, let the stillness grow, then said. 'What do you think of the proposition, Blade? Reckon you'd like a chance to get your hands on some real money and make these northern carpetbaggers see that we don't intend to stand for bein' trampled on.'

'You make it sound a durned sight easier than it is,' grunted the other, but from the tone of his voice, Ross could guess that he was half won over. He did not give Morelle the chance to butt in, but continued to press home his advantage. 'Ain't no reason why we should stay in this part of the territory. I figure one or two of us may be known around these parts. We could ride on west and north, where the main railroads are, ride openly into town and get enough information on the comings and goings of the trains to help us plan our hold-ups.'

'What do you reckon about it, Hank?' Blade turned to Morelle.

The other had been listening intently. Now he curled his lips into a derisive grin. 'He makes it sound all right. But it needs a bigger bunch than this to have a chance of pullin' a job like that.'

'Then you don't want in on it?' Ross asked pointedly. The other did not hesitate, but shook his head quickly, emphatically. 'Like I said, with my share of what we got from the Fort Carstairs bank I'm headin' south, over the border into Mexico. The law won't follow me there and I'll be livin' it up and enjoyin' myself when the rest of you have squandered your share of the money and are all swingin' from the end of a rope.'

'And you – Dane?' Ross turned to the tall, taciturn man with his back against the rock.

The other chewed thoughtfully on a piece

of wood for a moment, then shrugged. 'Reckon I'd miss all this if I rode south with Hank. Count me in on the deal.'

Bending forward, Hank looked up at Ross's tight face and sighed heavily. 'I'll split the money and then ride out, he said softly. 'That posse might still be around, tryin' to pick up our trail. I want to be well away from here by first light.'

'Suit yourself,' Ross said. He turned his head slowly to glance at the other men beneath the overhang. Clem did not count. Once they managed to get him to the doctor in Clarkson, they would see nothing more of him. He would drop out of their lives, just as Hank Morelle would once he took his share of the money and rode out. For a moment, it seemed that everything had happened so quickly his mind simply refused to take it all in. He had joined up with these men three days before, with no clear intention of following them; and now, he was virtually leading them. Certainly Morelle had been right about one thing. If they were to get into the big time, hold up the main trains on the railroad to the north, then they would need more men to help them, men who knew how to handle a gun, men he could trust. Once they pulled their first train robbery, their names would be splashed across the pages of every paper in every town along the frontier. There would be a price on their heads and they could look for men, anxious to join them, and then only too ready to betray them to the law.

The money in the wheat sacks was tipped into a pile by the side of the fire, the last blood-red rays of the sun touching the coin with a lambent flame. Ross took his share, stuffed it into one of the sacks and tied the top securely. By now, it was almost dark. Dane thrust more dry wood on to the fire, watched as it blazed up. The spot for the fire had been chosen carefully and although the flickering red glow was reflected from the rock wall, the overhang successfully prevented the reflection from spilling out over the surrounding area.

Morelle got heavily to his feet, hitched his gunbelt more tightly around his middle. He moved away from the fire, whistled up his horse and tied the wheat sack securely to the saddle. Bending, he tightened the cinch under the animal's belly.

'You really set on this, Hank?' Ross asked. He shifted his position a little on the ground. He didn't really like the idea of the other pulling out like this, just when they were getting started and inwardly he wondered how much the other's decision had been forced by his joining this band. He drew unhurriedly on his cigarette. Morelle drew his rifle from its scabbard, checked it, then pushed it back.

'I'm set on it,' be said stolidly. 'I've got a lot of livin' and drinkin' to do, and I aim to do it outside of this territory where the law can pop up at any time and start slugs whistlin' after me.'

He stepped into the saddle, turned to look down at Ross Halloran. 'I wish you luck with this venture of yours,' he said solemnly. 'I feel sure you're goin' to need it, all of you.'

His hand wrenched the horse's head about. Spurred heels dug into the animal's quivering flanks, urging it forward, hoofs clattering metallically on the hard rock of the smooth basin, sending it out into the clinging darkness. Ross sat motionless, listening to the brazen echoes dying swiftly away. So did the others, except for Clem. Sucking air in through his clenched teeth, his sweating face glistening in the glow of the fire, he said harshly. 'What the hell are you all staring for? Now will you get me into Clarkson to a doctor, or do you mean to leave me here to die?'

Clarkson was in darkness by the time they rode in. Walking their horses along the dusty main street, making little sound, they located the local doctor's house and roused him by knocking on the door with a gun-butt. The place was a small building of brick-faced lumber, sandwiched between a couple of general stores which were empty at that time of the night. Sullenly, noticing the guns which the men wore, the doctor extracted the bullet from Clem's shoulder, and bound up the wound.

'How bad is it, Doc?' Ross asked thinly. 'You figure he's well enough to be able to travel?'

'He's lost a lot of blood and that's not a good thing,' replied the other; 'but I can guess that you'll have to keep movin'.'

'Just what do you mean by that?' asked Dane sharply. He came upright from where he had been lounging near the doorway.

Harshly, the older man said: 'It's quite obvious to me who you are. You must be part of that band that held up the bank in Fort Carstairs. We got word of it late this afternoon. If you think you'll be able to outrun the law, you're wrong. The news was that Sheriff Tollinson died before a doctor could get to him. Now you're all wanted for murder as well as armed robbery.'

Without answering, Ross took a handful of coins from his pocket, placed them in a neat pile on the table. 'I figure that ought to pay for your trouble.'

For a moment, it looked as though the other intended picking up the money and throwing it back in his face, but he restrained himself, saying bitterly instead. 'This some of your proceeds from the robbery?'

'Take it or leave it,' Ross said tersely.

'It's better than a bullet in your back to stop you from talkin',' Dane put in coarsely. He motioned meaningly to the gun in his belt. 'But you haven't answered the question yet. Can he travel?'

'Hard to say how bad he's been hurt inside,' muttered the other after a brief pause. 'If any bone splinters touched the lung then there's nothin' I could do for him anyway. If they didn't, then he'll have a stiff shoulder for some weeks, but after that he should be all right. But travelling fast and hard on horseback won't help him none.'

'I'll risk that,' grunted Clem thinly. His face was still white, twisted with pain, and he wiped the back of his hand over his lips where some of the raw whisky he had been given to ease the pain during the probing for the bullet, had dribbled down his chin. He swung his legs weakly to the floor, tried to stand unaided, would have fallen if Ross had not stepped forward quickly and put an arm around his middle.

'I'll be OK,' he muttered hoarsely. 'Just get me on my horse and let's get out of here before there's a posse on our tail. They'll sure enough be after us once it gets light.'

'What do we do about this *hombre?*' asked Dane, jerking a thumb in the direction of the elderly doctor. 'Leave him here to tell everybody that we've been here and that one of us has been badly hurt? The posse would sure like to know about that.'

Ross reached a sudden decision. 'We tie him up and lock him in the back room,' he said tautly. The idea of killing someone in cold blood was abhorrent to him.

5

Pecos Crossing

Across the wide stretch of the Arkansas river, three men rode north, riding in the opposite direction to that in which the law would expect them to ride. Eight days had passed since they had ridden out of Clarkson, eight days of desert and rivers in flood, mountains and thick stands of timber, heat and cold. Clem Toner had been left in Twin Creeks on the third day out. Loss of blood and a shoulder burning with infection had forced him to withdraw. Now there were just the three of them, trailweary riders who dozed in their saddles as they put another and still another mile behind them.

Another day's ride and they would reach the railhead at Abilene. Sitting forward in the saddle, Dane Whitfield could almost smell the gold that lay somewhere ahead of them. His brain kept whispering that there would be more than enough for all of them and suddenly, a great eagerness took hold of him. Gold hunger was stronger than the weariness and the food hunger that gnawed at his belly. As he rode, he studied the land around them. Here, it was a dry, arid country in which very little grew but the brown scrub that whispered eerily whenever the hot wind blew through the stiff branches, rustling them with a sound that resembled the last, whimpering breath of the dying. He had seen many men die during his service with the Confederate Army; and inwardly, he tried to rub out the memory of that, but the morning wind and the dust that whined through the scrub kept him constantly reminded of it.

For a moment, he wondered about Hank Morelle. Dane reflected that there had been something strange about the way Hank had pulled out like that, when there had been this chance of getting their hands on more wealth than any of them had ever dreamed of in their lives. Until this man Halloran had joined them Hank had made no mention of leaving the band. Had he foreseen that there was big trouble ahead for them if they fell in with Halloran's ideas? He stole a quick, sideways glance at the man who rode just in front of him, sitting tall and square in the saddle, his face fixed and hard, just as it had always been since they had pulled out of Clarkson.

There seemed no doubt that Halloran was nursing some big grudge against the railroad, or maybe against the North in general. He seemed little interested in the money. It was as if he had a long-standing feud between himself and the Northerners, something that had not died when the war had ended, which had, indeed, been fanned into a brighter flame since then. He was a hard man to understand. There was something deep inside him that seldom came up to the surface where another man might see it and recognize it for what it was. This desperate urge that drove him on might, at some time in the future, be the undoing of him. It might bring rashness in its wake and in their business that could be fatal.

Inwardly, he told himself that if they managed to pull off half a dozen hold-ups, then he too would move south, follow Hank into Mexico where he might be outside the range of the law. It seemed true that the gratifications which a man craved the most always seemed to be just out of reach.

They made a rough ascent, came out on a long, low ledge of rock that stretched for almost a mile in either direction. Ross reined up his mount, turned in the saddle, staring intently into the dust haze behind them. The wind was louder up here, shrilling in rising crescendoes over the tumbled rock formations etched into fluted columns of stone by long geological ages of dust and wind.

'You know this country, Ross?' Dane asked, resting his elbows on the pommel.

'Only from five or six years back. Things could have changed a little since then. Towns get bigger and there are others thrown up almost overnight. Now that the railroad has come to Abilene, they'll be drivin' their herds up here for shipment back East. I figure there's plenty of gold bein' carried on this stretch of railroad and if I remember right, there's a little place about ten miles east of Abilene called Pecos Crossing. The trains sometimes stop there to pick up mail and the odd passenger.'

Dane nodded his head thoughtfully, his eyes speculative. 'So that's the best place for the hold-up.'

'Right. But first we have to find out when they'll be carryin' gold on the train and when it's due to reach Pecos Crossing.'

'How do you figure on doin' that?'

'We'll pick a spot about a couple of miles

out of Abilene where we can hole up for a few days without attractin' any unwanted attention. I'll ride into Abilene and ask around.'

'You plumb crazy!' muttered Blade thinly. 'Who'll talk to you like that?'

Ross smiled thinly. 'That's the big trouble with you two,' he said evenly. 'You never think ahead. With some of the money I've got, I should be able to get me a decent rig so that I can pass for a cattle buyer from back East. Folk will talk to a man they know has money.'

'Then what?'

'We'll make our plans once we get that information. Might even be best if I was to travel on the train. There could be guards on board who might give us trouble unless we could take care of 'em right away.'

'Makes sense, I reckon,' said Dane finally. He nodded. 'Let's find this place where we can rest up. These last few days have been some of the worst I've known.'

Abilene was a swiftly growing metropolis, far larger and more important now than in the years when Ross Halloran had known it. There were blocks of stores on either side of the main street and even the streets which led off from it were wide, compared with those found in other towns along the trail. Being so far west, it had fewer buildings of brick than smaller towns further to the East, and in places, where the roads could become rivers of dust or wide stretches of sticky brown mud depending on the weather, the wooden boardwalks were two or three feet above the level of the street.

Ross did not ride on into the centre of the town, but put up in a small boarding house near the edge of the place. Here, his clothing was not too conspicuous. There were many men who rode in from the vast plains to the south, herding their cattle to the railhead. But if he was to get the information he needed, then he would have to alter his appearance considerably, and he set about doing this at once, buying an entirely new outfit.

Dressed in grey-striped trousers and a Prince Albert coat and heavy silk shirt, he knew that he would have little trouble in passing for a wealthy beef buyer from the East. During the next two days, he took to walking downtown, making himself known, using his own name here.

On the third day, he went out to the stockyard that crowded in on the gleaming rails. The lumber had curled in the heat of the sun and much of it was still unpainted, but it was there and almost every pen was full of longhorn cattle brought up from the great plains of Texas along the newly opened Chisholm Trail, the trail along which more than a million head of cattle would be brought to the railhead during the next few years. But very little of Ross's attention went on the cattle, lowing and bawling in the pens. He mingled with the black-coated men from the North, his southern drawl standing out a little among the Yankee twang.

The man nearest to him, tall, his skin slightly yellowed, introduced himself to Halloran. 'My name is Cal Rawlins. You here to buy beef, Mister—'

'Halloran,' said Ross. He nodded. 'It may seem strange that a man from the north of Texas is in Abilene looking for beef, but I'm employed by the J.G. McCoy Company from Illinois. My first visit here.'

'You'll find plenty of cattle here, Mister Halloran,' said the other, his tone polite, almost friendly. 'But I wouldn't delay if I were you. There are a lot of buyers here too. The price is between twenty-five and thirty dollars a head. If they don't get another herd here soon, it's likely to go even higher.'

'There are plenty of cattle in Texas,' Ross said quietly. He let his gaze wander on the milling animals in the pens.

'I understand it's a hard and dangerous trail up from Texas.'

Ross looked blank for a moment, then nodded. He stared thoughtfully at Rawlins. Then he shook his head. 'Not having ridden it, I couldn't say.' He rubbed his chin. 'I'll have to wire details to my Company. They'll then have to send on the gold here if I'm to put in a bid.'

The other nodded musingly. 'I'm a business man myself, Halloran,' he said with a faint laugh, 'but it seems to me a strange way to do business.'

Ross eyed him sharply, made to say something, paused as the other went on quickly. 'By that I mean they send gold out here to pay for the cattle we buy, and at the same time, it goes back East whenever the banks in Abilene want to send it out for safer keeping.'

Ross raised his brows a little. 'Isn't it safe in the bank vaults in Abilene?' he inquired innocently.

The other smiled thinly. 'They say this is still the frontier with the West, Mister Halloran. There have been some robberies

109

during the past few months, most of them further south than Abilene, I'll admit. But even here, I doubt if we would be entirely safe from them. These gangs of outlaws are getting more and more daring, and stronger. In several cases, the law seems to have been utterly helpless.'

'And what about the trains themselves?' He smiled faintly. 'Surely they must be a temptation to any outlaws?'

'That's perfectly true, but there are always guards and Pinkerton men travelling on board the trains whenever they carry a shipment of gold or currency. Besides, only the banks know when there is going to be gold on any of the trains.' He lowered his voice conspiratorially. 'If you want my advice, Mister Halloran, I would arrange any transfer of funds through one of the banks. It's much safer that way.'

'Thanks. I think I'll take your advice.'

Moving away, Ross walked around the pens for a further twenty minutes, remaining inconspicuous. The dust and stench and the loud-throated bellows of the cattle were in his ears and nostrils. The sun was now high in the heavens, with the heat head lifting swiftly, climbing to the point where it was almost unbearable. The clothing he wore became an encumbrance to him and he felt the sweat trickling down his back and forehead. A snorting locomotive sounded a low, wailing whistle. Cattle were herded along the gleaming rails that shone like burnished silver in the bright glare of the sun; forced up into the wooden box cars which would transport them a thousand miles across a continent.

Ross watched for a while and then turned away, walked back into the main street until he came to the imposing façade of the bank. For a moment there was a faint thrill of apprehension in him, then he forced it down. Going inside, he went up to the counter, his eyes taking in everything instinctively.

The clerk glanced up as he paused in front of the teller's booth, then said in a quiet, respectful voice: 'Can I do anything for you, sir?'

'I'd like to discuss some business in private with the manager if that's possible.'

The clerk glanced over his shoulder. Following the direction of the other's gaze, Ross saw the tall, thin-faced man seated in one of the small sectioned areas with a glass screen dividing it from the rest of the building. This, he guessed, was the manager.

'I'll see if Mister Mulvaney is available, sir,'

he said politely. 'May I have your name?'

'Ross Halloran. I'm a cattle buyer.'

The other nodded, made his way through the small gate at the back of the booth and whispered a few words in the manager's ear. Ross noticed, out of the corner of his eye, that both men had lifted their heads and were studying him closely. Then he saw the manager nod his head slowly.

The clerk came back, held a door in the counter open for him. 'If you'll just come through Mister Halloran,' he said.

Ross nodded, walked through. Mulvaney got to his feet and held out a hand to him. 'My clerk tells me that you have some important business you wish to discuss with me in private, Mister Halloran. Please sit down.' He motioned to the chair in front of the long, low desk.

When Ross was seated, he went on: 'Now, what is it that the bank can do for you? Arrange a loan, or do you wish to make a deposit?'

Ross settled himself back in his chair. He took the cigar which the other offered him, lit it and waited until it was going before he said: 'I'm here to buy cattle, Mister Mulvaney. I've just come from the stockyards and I met an old friend of mine there, name of Rawlins.'

He saw the look of recognition which came into the banker's eyes, knew that the other's name was well known to him as he had guessed that it might have been. This made an excellent introduction for himself. 'I was asking him about getting gold through to Abilene and perhaps out again. He advised me to see you and arrange all of this through your agency here.'

Mulvaney placed the tips of his fingers together, let his keen-eyed gaze wander over the other. Evidently, he liked what he saw, for there was no suspicion on his face as he nodded and said: 'We'll be only too pleased to make all of the necessary arrangements for you, Mister Halloran. The bank has been established here for less than a couple of years, but we already have arrangements with the railroad.' He pulled a sheaf of papers towards him, riffled through them quickly.

'As you'll understand, shipments of gold are carried infrequently. We cannot take chances. Too many banks have been held up by outlaws in the past few months and there is evidence that they may be switching their activities to the railroads and stage lines.'

'But surely you have guards on the trains whenever gold or currency is being carried?'

113

'Oh certainly. But we also take the precaution of making shipments on an irregular basis.' His lips twisted faintly into a frosty smile. 'We sometimes put guards on the trains when there is no gold on board to throw them off the scent. I think I can say that it is our proud boast that no one has robbed the railroad of any of our gold during the time that we have been established here.'

Ross smiled grimly to himself. This was certainly not the time to enlighten the other.

'Can you tell me when the next train will be arriving in Abilene with gold on board? I can then wire my Company and they can make the necessary arrangements in Illinois.' For a moment he thought that he had broached the subject too suddenly. He forced himself to remain casual, staring down at the glowing tip of the cigar, the blue tendrils of smoke curling up to the ceiling.

But Mulvaney made no comment, continued to search through the papers. Then he glanced up, his long forefinger pressed against the page. 'If you can wire them; right away, Mister Halloran, they may be able to get it on to the train this evening. It's due in here at ten o'clock tomorrow night. Will that be soon enough for you?' Another faint smile creased his thin features. 'I know that you buyers like to be ready to bid as soon as possible. There was a large herd came in a few days ago and, by now, most of the bidding will have been made. I'm not sure when the next herd is due.'

'If I can get the money here by tomorrow evening, I feel sure that I can make some arrangements today,' Ross said, getting to his feet. 'You've been very helpful.'

Blade sat on the edge of the rocky outcrop and wiped the sweat from his face with the ragged sleeve of his jacket. He picked up the mug of hot coffee and stared across at Ross, brows lowered into a straight line. 'You sure this banker fella told you right, Ross? The train is due in Abilene tomorrow night at ten?'

'That's right. I'm sure he was tellin' the truth. Now we've got to decide on the best plan for gettin' our hands on it.'

'There are only the three of us now,' Dane pointed out meaningly. 'It won't be easy.'

Ross said earnestly: 'They won't be expectin' trouble. This is the way I figure it. There's a place some fifteen miles east of Pecos Crossing where I could get on the train and travel with it. I'll get my ticket through to

Abilene to make things even less suspicious. Once I'm on board, I'll locate the gold and the whereabouts of the guards. You two ride into Pecos Crossing fifteen minutes before the train is due, cut the wires from the stations so that they can't give any warnin' and then set up the red signal lamps to stop the train. One of you take the fireman and engineer. The other get on board and come with me.'

'It would be easier if we had more men with us,' Dane complained.

'Maybe so, but we don't have anybody else and I wouldn't take on another man unless I could be absolutely sure of him and in the short time we have, that's out of the question.'

Dane shrugged, said nothing more. It was Blade who spoke up. 'When we get the gold, always reckonin' that everythin' will be OK, what then?'

'You'll bring a third horse with you for me. We'll head north into the timber. They'll be expectin' us to go south and if there is any pursuit, most of it will be headed away from us.'

'Sounds all right,' agreed Blade somewhat reluctantly.

'Just do as I say and it will be all right,'

Ross said savagely. 'This time we're goin' to give the railroad somethin' to think about; somethin' they won't forget in a hurry.'

The station at Pecos Crossing was a single building that ran alongside the tracks, a ticket office standing side by side with the telegraph office. There was nobody in the ticket office when the two men rode up, dismounting while they were still some distance from the station, going forward the rest of the way on foot, making no noise in the ankle-deep dust. The settlement of Pecos Crossing was almost a mile away, a tiny cluster of adobe huts, half lost in the dimness of twilight. There was nobody in sight on the low platform outside the wicket and only the agent was on duty, seated in the chair behind the telegraph instruments, his feet up on top of the low desk. Once the westbound train for Abilene passed through he would be able to go off duty, to lock up the place and go home. The wind that whistled around the building was becoming chill now that the sun had gone down and he was not looking forward to the long walk into Pecos Crossing.

Taking his watch from the pocket of his waistcoat, he checked it for the dozenth time, then slipped it back. Another fifteen minutes, almost to the dot before the train came in. Fortunately there were no passengers and he would not have to light the lanterns and set them out near the track. It was seldom that anyone took this train into Abilene from here.

It was then that he heard the sound of footsteps outside the office and muttered a faint curse under his breath as he swung his legs to the floor and heaved himself to his feet. It seemed he was wrong about there being no passengers going on into Abilene. Probably some cattlemen anxious to get into town on the last train. Certainly there was nothing in Pecos Crossing to keep them there for the night.

He reached the door of the telegraph office, then stepped back a couple of paces as a heavy Colt was thrust into his stomach.

'Get back inside there and keep your hands lifted,' snarled the tall man with the gun. He dug the barrel more roughly into the agent's middle, bringing a gasp of pain to the other's lips. The man lifted his hands at once, moving back into the room. Standing there, ashen-faced, with his eyes switching from the man in front of him to the other, shorter man who came in, looked about him for a moment, then pulled a pair of wire cutters from his pocket and proceeded to snip the wires that snaked from the telegraph instrument on the table. Wrenching the transmitting key from the instrument, he thrust it into his pocket, then nodded to his companion. His voice was muffled by the linen duster he wore over the lower half of his face as he said: 'I reckon that's that taken care of.'

'Good. Then we'll get the warnin' signals set.' He turned to the agent. 'What signals do you set out there for the Abilene train to stop here?'

'But no signals are set unless there are passengers to be carried,' quavered the other. He seemed unable to take his glance from the gun in Blade's hand.

'There'll be a couple of extra passengers tonight,' snapped the other. 'Two that they ain't bargained for. Now get those signals set and don't try anythin' funny or I'll put a bullet into you and finish the job myself.' It was important that the agent should not realize how dependent they were on him to set the correct signals. The more he thought himself to be dispensable, the more he could be trusted to do the job properly.

The agent took a further glance at the gun

in Blade's hand, saw the barrel laid un-waveringly on him and decided against making any attempt to reach the scattergun kept under the desk for any emergencies such as this. He gave a brief nod, went to the ticket office and brought out three red lanterns, then moved over to set the signals. Once the lanterns were set out on the edge of the rails, Dane locked the agent inside the telegraph office after tying and gagging him.

In the darkness, Blade stared along the railroad where it stretched away into the distance. Here, the country was flat as far as the eye could see, with the dry, dusty prairies on either side. There was no sign yet of the train, but it still needed ten minutes before it was due to arrive at Pecos Crossing. It had taken only five minutes to prepare every-thing for the stopping of the express at the station.

Half an hour earlier, Ross Halloran had boarded the train at Caracoa. It had not proved difficult to work his way along the central aisles to the end of the coach immediately in front of the luggage car at the rear of the train. He made his way out on to the observation platform at the back and took out a cigar, biting off the end, then lighting it, puffing on it reflectively in the fast-fading light. The conductor was still inside the express car, but there had been two men inside the last of the passenger cars whom he had instantly guessed to be Pinkerton men. There were tell-tale bulges under their coats indicating that they were armed. If he could stay on the observation platform until the train came to a standstill at Pecos Crossing and then take care of those two men, he felt sure that Blade and Dane, between them, should be able to deal with the engineer and fireman, and also the messenger and conductor in the express car. He expected little, if any, trouble from the passengers. There were few on the train and none looked the type to butt into gunplay simply for the sake of proving himself to be a hero.

Moving to the rail, he peered along the track, trying to make out the signals which ought to have been set by now, if Blade and Dane had done their job properly. He tried not to think of the many things which could have gone wrong, which could still go wrong. If they got away with this, they would undeniably have to lie low for a while. Every lawman, every Pinkerton and railroad detective would be hunting them down. The territory would be too hot even for them.

He felt the rush of cold air in his face bring the tears into his eyes, so that his vision became blurred and it was impossible for him to see anything properly. Drawing himself back out of reach of the wind, he forced himself to wait patiently. Through the small window nearby, he was able to peer into the coach and watch the two men who sat just beyond the door. They were seated side by side now, deep in conversation. They looked like men who knew how to handle themselves and he felt for the gun at his waist, fingers closing instinctively around the butt as he heard the moaning wail of the locomotive, drifting down to him on the wind. At almost the same time, there was the shuddering squeal of brakes being applied and he felt the change in motion as he put out his left hand, holding tightly to the rail.

Leaning a little to one side, he peered along the track once more and this time he caught sight of the red warning signals gleaming faintly in the darkness ahead. The train was already jarring to a standstill with the grating of metal on metal and the shrill hiss of escaping steam.

6

A Time for Guns

The shot that rang out near the front of the train carried loudly down to the rear coach. Jerking the gun from its holster, Ross pressed himself close to the end of the coach. A second later, the door was flung open and the two Pinkerton men came out on to the observation platform. One of them moved to cross over to the express car, froze instantly as Ross snapped: 'Hold it right there! Both of you!'

The first man stopped, then lifted his hands slowly. But the second, almost without thinking, suddenly swung, aiming a clenched fist at Ross's head. The movement nearly took him by surprise. Ducking swiftly, he rode the force of the blow, but the man's body, falling off balance, crashed against him, almost bearing him over the low rail and down on to the track below. Savagely, Ross fought to stay upright, knowing that once he went over, he would be finished and any chance of pulling off the robbery would be gone. Desperately, he kicked up with his leg, caught the man in the groin, heard him gasp with agony and fall back slightly, but he had already thrown his arms around Ross's middle to save himself from staggering completely off balance and now he continued to hang on.

Out of the corner of his eye, Ross saw the other man moving in, tugging at the gun in his belt. Almost without thinking, exerting every ounce of strength in his right hand, Ross swung his own gun up, squeezed the trigger, saw the man's face glare redly in the crimson bloom of the muzzle flash. The twisted features contorted violently as the slug caught the man high in the chest, pitching him backwards as if he had been slammed by a mighty hand. He dropped the gun he had pulled from his belt. It struck the observation platform with a dull thud a moment before the Pinkerton man slewed round, clutching at his chest, his shoulders bouncing off the low rail at his back.

The man holding on to Ross's waist swung him around with a sudden surge of desperate strength. The move brought Ross's arm striking hard against the metal rail and the gun dropped from his numbed fingers. He could feel the other's arms tightening convulsively as the man strove to snap his spine in a bear hug. He could sense his ribs bending under the tremendous strain and struggled to force himself upright, knowing that once the other man bent him back against the rail, it would be the end of him.

There was a dull roaring in his ears, the sound of his own blood throbbing at the back of his temples, racing along his veins. His vision was becoming more and more blurred and there seemed to be a red haze dancing in front of his eyes. Although Ross was somewhat taller than his opponent, he did not have the man's brute physical strength and he also knew that with every second that passed, the danger to him and to his two companions now somewhere on the train would be increased. Soon, the messenger and the conductor would come bursting out of the express car and he knew they would both be armed.

Sucking air down into his tortured lungs, he forced clearness into his mind. For a second, he allowed himself to go completely limp, slumping against the other and, in spite of himself, the man relaxed his hold slightly. Whether he thought that Ross was finished or not, it was hard to tell. But this relaxation of his effort, slight though it was, was enough for Ross. Savagely, he swung up his right fist, hit the man full on the mouth, felt his knuckles hammer with a satisfying solidity on the other's face. Blood gushed down the man's shirt front and he half fell back, arms swinging limply by his sides. Then, almost without pause, he came boring in again. A hard blow caught Ross on the side of the head and he staggered under the force of it. The edge of the rail hit him hard in the small of the back, so that he almost overbalanced. Faintly, he was aware of the glow of triumph in the man's eyes, saw him rush forward now, certain of victory. Dazed as he was, Ross realized he had only one chance. In the split second before the other reached him, he ducked and rolled to one side. With a roar of bull-like rage, the other stumbled past him, his arms outflung. Swinging round, Ross hit him with the flat of his hand on the back of the neck as he went forward, pitching him over the rail and on to the track below. Going forward, sucking air down into his heaving chest, Ross stared down at the man lying on the rails. His arms and legs were outflung and his head was twisted at a curious angle. He did not move and Ross knew then that his neck was broken, that even if it had not been broken by the force of the rabbit punch he had delivered, the fall had certainly killed him.

He scrabbled on the floor of the platform for a moment until he found his gun, then moved to the edge of the rail, leaned out and stared along the line. There was a man running along the side of the train and a second later, as the other loomed out of the darkness, he saw that it was Dane.

Swiftly, the other swung himself up on to the observation platform. He gave the two bodies a cursory glance. 'Trouble?' he asked tersely.

'Some,' Ross admitted wryly. He gulped air down into his lungs, feeling it burn his raw throat on the way down. 'Blade has got the agent locked up and he's coverin' the fireman and engineer. They shouldn't give us any trouble.'

'Let's get across to the express car.' Ross motioned towards the last coach in the train. Swiftly, they eased their way over to the far observation platform, swung themselves up. The door opened almost as they got to it and the startled face of the conductor appeared in the opening. He held a shotgun in his hands and relaxed a little as he caught sight of Ross, evidently mistaking him in the excitement for one of the Pinkerton men.

'I thought I heard shots,' he gasped hoarsely. 'What's happenin'.'

Ross thrust the heavy Colt sharply into the man's stomach as Dane reached over and almost gently removed the shotgun from the other's grasp.

'Get back inside,' Ross said. 'Do just like we tell you and nobody is goin' to get hurt.'

The other staggered back, air whooshing through his tightly clenched teeth as the barrel of the gun ground into his soft parts. Over the conductor's shoulder, Ross saw the messenger standing in the middle of the express car. There were two lanterns swinging from the roof, giving enough light for him to see that these were the only two men in the coach. There were several wooden boxes stacked along one side and a robust-looking metal safe in one corner.

'Where are the keys to the safe?' Ross demanded harshly. 'Hand them over. Pronto!'

The other was shaking visibly. Swallowing hard, he said in a low, husky tone, 'We don't carry keys to a through safe like that. They have them at Abilene.'

'He's lyin',' said Dane thinly. He stepped

forward, levelling his gun at the other's head, his finger tightening on the trigger. 'Give me a minute and I'll soon get the truth out of him.'

Ross sighed. 'I reckon he's tellin' the truth,' he said finally. 'It's the sort of thing they'd do to prevent a robbery and the safe is too big and heavy for us to carry even if we managed to get it off the train. Besides, we'd need a charge of dynamite to get it open. A bullet won't make an impression on that metal.'

'What do we do then?'

'Take a look in those boxes yonder,' Ross said. While he had been speaking, he had noticed the way in which the messenger had been unable to prevent his gaze from flicking in the direction of the wooden boxes piled along the wall.

Dane hesitated, then shrugged, moved to the nearest box, seized it by one corner and heaved with all of his strength. It was obvious that the box was far heavier than it looked.

It tilted, then crashed on to the floor of the car, shattering as the fragile wood splintered. A pile of gold coins spilled out, gleaming dully in the light from the overhead lanterns.

Dane drew in his breath in a whistling

gasp through his teeth. Going down on one knee, he ran his fingers through the pile, then looked up. 'Could be that the rest of these boxes are the same,' he said excitedly.

'Drag them over to the door and heave them out on to the track,' Ross ordered. 'We'll load up the contents into the sacks as soon as we've got this train away.'

Dane hesitated for a moment, then did as he was told. He had one wheat sack knotted around his middle and pulled it off once he had finished tipping the other boxes out through the door. Swiftly, he scooped the pile of coins into the sack, tied the end in a secure knot, then dropped it out after the boxes.

'All right,' said Ross sharply. 'Now get along the track and tell Blade to order the engineer to start up the train and move it out. If they don't keep goin', I'll drill the conductor and messenger.'

'You stayin' on the train?' asked Dane incredulously.

'Ain't no reason for the engineer to think otherwise, is there?'

Dane grinned. 'I guess not.' He lowered himself out of the car. Ross heard him moving along the side of the train. The conductor shifted his position slightly, then froze as Ross swung the heavy Colt to cover him. Sweat stood out on his face, gleaming to the yellow lamplight.

'Just hold it there, or I may get the idea that you're tryin' to reach a gun and I might just pull this trigger.'

'You won't get away with this, you know,' said the other harshly. 'There will be Pinkerton men and the sheriff's posse on your trail before you can get a couple of miles from here. Where do you think you're going to run to with that gold?'

'That's our affair,' Ross said in an icy tone. He leaned himself back against the wall of the express car close to the door, throwing an occasional glance down to where the boxes and Dane's wheat sack lay beside the rails.

For a moment, he wondered how much there was down there, then put the thought out of his mind as the locomotive blew off steam with a great hiss and the train began to move, slowly at first, then gathering speed. Ross braced himself on the edge of the car, then threw a swift glance at the two men, their eyes fixed on him.

'Turn and face the wall,' he ordered sharply. 'Quickly!'

They obeyed reluctantly. Once their backs

were turned to him, he thrust the Colt into his belt, paused for a moment poised on the edge of the door, then jumped out into the night. Even though the train was travelling only slowly, he hit the ground with a shuddering impact that jarred all the way up his legs and into his body. For a moment, he lay winded, then somehow thrust himself to his feet. The train was moving away into the distance, the great beam of the headlight cutting through the darkness as it curved away around the bend in the track beyond Pecos Crossing.

Dane and Blade came running back down the track. The whole attack on the train from the moment that the locomotive had ground to a halt at the tiny wayside station had taken less than ten minutes. Blade stared down at the dark shapes of the boxes and the wheat sack, then bent to examine them more closely. When he looked up, his face a dull grey blur in the dimness, he said tightly: 'There must be close on fifty or sixty thousand dollars here, Ross. We sure made us a killin' tonight.'

Ross nodded swiftly. 'Let's get away from here before the engineer stops that train. The conductor will be makin' his way forward to the engine this minute.'

It was the work of five minutes to transfer the coins into the remaining wheat sacks. By the time this was done, there were six of them, so heavy that a man could barely hold two of them at once. Tying them securely to their saddles, they mounted up and headed north into the wind-blown darkness. Not until they had put several miles between themselves and the railroad, when they were deep inside the timber that grew on the low foothills of the tall mountains, did they ease up, finally halting in a small clearing where they spread one of their blankets on the ground and counted out the money. It came to a little more than sixty-seven thousand dollars.

Ross sat back on his haunches, stared at the other two. 'Once we've divided it out, we'd better split up. There's goin' to be one almighty fuss about this once they hear of it in Abilene. This part of the territory won't be too healthy for us for three or four months at least. Once that conductor mentions me, they'll soon tie me in with the man who started askin' questions at the bank about how the gold was bein' brought into Abilene.'

'This could set us all up for life if we made it over the border into Mexico,' said Dane in a hushed tone. 'There's more money here than I ever thought existed in the whole of the state.'

Ross shook his head. 'This is only the beginnin',' he said softly. 'Once the heat is off our trail, we'll go on. Soon there won't be a stretch of railroad in the whole country that hasn't heard of us.'

'How do we keep in touch until you're ready to pull another robbery?' asked Blade. He ran the tip of his tongue around his dry lips.

Ross thought about that, then said: 'We'll all meet in Dodge three months from now. That ought to give us time. But be careful. Whatever you do, don't start spendin' money in a big way. We don't dare underestimate the Pinkerton men.'

When Kirby Hilger arrived in Abilene, the news of the robbery was three days old. Alighting from the stage, he made his way at once to the local office of the Pinkerton Agency in the town. He did not like the look of Abilene. The towns of Kansas were ugly when compared with those of the East; their buildings all weatherbeaten, squat and too functional to his eyes, square and unpainted, or where there was paint, it was blistered and peeling from long exposure to the fierce sunlight. Even in the light of the late afternoon, the buildings still had a grim and forbidding look about them, ugly and inhospitable.

He felt badly in need of a wash and a drink and some food in him, but he was a man who always put business before his own pleasures, which was why he had been chosen by the Agency to come out here and take charge of the investigation into the robbery in which the outlaws had got away with more than sixty thousand dollars in gold coin.

Pushing the door of the outer office open, he went inside. The clerk seated behind the desk jerked his head up in surprise, staring at him for a moment, obviously trying to determine who he might be, before he started asking any pertinent questions.

Hilger wasted no time. 'My name is Kirby Hilger,' he said and his voice had an edge which the clerk noticed at once. 'I've been sent to take charge here. Where can I find Leary?'

'He's through in the other office, Mister Hilger,' stammered the clerk hastily. Getting to his feet, he led the way to the other door, rapped sharply on it, then opened it and stood on one side to allow Hilger to precede him into the room.

Leary was a short, balding man who looked as if he had been athletic at one time, but had now let himself run to fat. He placed his cigar in the tray in front of him and heaved himself to his feet, extending his hand.

'I've been expecting you, Hilger,' he said affably. 'They said you would be coming down to take charge. I only regret that you had to make this trip, but the trouble is that–'

'The trouble seems to be that someone here has been sleeping on his job,' said Hilger sharply. He shook the other's hand briefly, then sat down in the chair in front of the desk. 'I shall want as full a report as possible on this – unfortunate affair – and then I shall decide on the steps which are to be taken.'

Leary sank down into his chair, waved a hand at the clerk and waited until the other had left the room, closing the door behind him, before bringing out a bottle and a couple of glasses. He poured a glass for each of them, tossed his down in a single gulp without blinking an eyelid, then poured another, sat back and contemplated the amber liquid in his glass for a long moment before speaking.

'I've made inquiries in Abilene since the robbery. I've no doubt that the leader of this gang of outlaws was a man who came here two days before it happened, giving his name as Ross Halloran. He passed himself off as a cattle buyer from back East, asked around the stockyards and then at the bank about trains which brought in gold and took it back East again. No one suspected anything about him. He learned from the bank that this train was due to arrive in Abilene that night and he must have been the one on the train from Caracoa, the man who killed our two agents guarding the shipment.'

'How many men were in the band?'

'According to the conductor and messenger, there were just the three of them.'

Hilger nodded. The other had learned a little more than he had expected. Much of the ground work appeared to have been done. Whether the name this man had used had been his own or one he had borrowed for the purpose, he did not know. It was very seldom that outlaws used their real names so he was forced to go on the assumption that it had been a false one. He sipped the whiskey slowly, feeling a little of the warmth come back into his body. He still felt weary and dusty from the long stage journey. Four days by stage was enough to weary any man to the marrow. Maybe that was why he could see nothing good in Abilene. He threw a calculating glance at the man behind the desk, noticing the way the flesh on his face clung to his cheek bones. He smiled a little without mirth. This was probably the first time that anything like this had happened to the Pinkerton Agency here in Abilene and Leary was unsure how to handle it. When a man was worrying as Leary obviously had been, he got a little tarnished-looking, a little thinner in the features than usual. It was the price a man paid for being in this business. He knew inwardly that sooner or later, he was going to end up looking like this man.

He finished his drink, feeling the spirit bite at his stomach. Leary put his empty glass on the desk, reached out with his hand for the bottle to pour another, then obviously decided against it, for he let his hand fall to his side and shook his head slowly, a trifle sadly.

'The trouble with this town, with this part of the territory, is that it begins to eat at you, slowly, so that you don't notice it until it's too goddamned late. Then there ain't a durned thing you can do about it.'

'Pull yourself together,' Hilger snapped harshly. 'Headquarters expect us to find these men, run them down to earth, and get as much of that gold back as possible. The longer we take, the less gold there's still likely to be.'

Leary shook his head slowly. 'They'll have split up long before this,' he said with conviction. 'You'll never find them.' He shifted his weight unconsciously in his chair.

'We'll find them,' Hilger said quietly. 'The organization we have is so widespread that they don't have a chance of eluding our net for long. Sooner or later, they'll meet up again to plan another robbery, these men always do; and when that happens, I shall be ready for them, if we haven't caught them before.'

'I hope you're right, but I reckon you may be pushing your luck a little too far if you're hoping for that.'

Hilger got slowly to his feet. 'Naturally I shall have every help from you and the men working here,' he said. The way he put it, it was obviously a statement of fact and not a question.

Leary nodded his head. 'That goes without saying,' he muttered. This time he did pour himself the third drink, drank it off in two quick gulps, his lips twisting in a sharp grimace as the liquor hit the back of his throat on the way down.

'Good. Now perhaps you can tell me who the sheriff is in Abilene, and then where I can get myself a decent room.'

'You'll find Sheriff Crowden in the office fifty yards or so along the street,' Leary said. 'As for a room, I'd recommend the hotel directly opposite here. It's clean and comfortable.'

'Thanks,' Hilger nodded again, went out, leaving Leary seated behind the desk, staring moodily in front of him, seeing nothing in particular. The other had the sudden feeling that with the arrival of this man from Headquarters, things were not going to be the same in Abilene as far as the Pinkerton organization was concerned.

Sheriff Crowden was a grizzled, big-fisted man with narrow, suspicious eyes that believed nothing and a thin-lipped, tough-set mouth. He said nothing when Hilger walked into his office but continued to sit in the high-backed chair behind the desk, sipping from the cup of steaming coffee.

'Help yourself to a cup,' Crowden said, indicating the pot on the stove. The sheriff's steady gaze brightened a little as he watched Hilger move to the stove, pour himself a cup of coffee, then come back and sit down facing him. 'Now, what's on your mind?'

Hilger felt some of his tiredness vanish under the stimulus of the black coffee. 'My name's Kirby Hilger,' he said softly. 'I've been sent here by the Pinkerton organization to investigate the robbery three days ago when close on seventy thousand dollars in gold was taken from the train at Pecos Crossing.'

The sheriff's gaze turned bright and appraising. 'I sort of figured they might be sendin' somebody along to look into it.' His tone implied that he thought this to be purely a case for the law, of which he was the duly elected representative, and that he resented any outsider horning in on the job, although at the same time, he did not wish to turn down any help that he might get.

'How far have you got, Sheriff? I understand from Leary at the office that the man who led the outlaws probably went under the name of Ross Halloran. Whether or not that is his real name is of little

141

concern. The point is that we can probably get a pretty good likeness of him drawn out for a poster.'

Crowden smiled a trifle sardonically. 'I've already done that, Mister Hilger,' he said. He dug into the drawer of his desk, came out with a roll of posters and laid one down on the desk in front of him, smoothing it out with his hands. 'This is the best we could do, but I've shown it to the bank manager, the clerk and several passengers on the train, as well as the conductor and messenger. They all agree it's a good likeness.'

'So we're agreed on that,' Hilger said. He stared down, at the face of the man in the poster. Somehow, the other did not look like the usual run of men who turned outlaw, leading these killers on a rampage throughout the territory. There was a look of sensitiveness about the face which he found hard to associate with a ruthless killer. Yet this was undeniably how it was and he knew that his first impression of the man must have been wrong.

'I formed a posse as soon as the train arrived in Abilene and I heard of the hold-up,' Crowden went on patiently. 'We managed to follow their trail a couple of miles to the north, then lost it among the rocks. It's rough country up there and they must have known that when they made their plans.'

'Why do you say that?' inquired Hilger sharply.

'Because in ordinary circumstances, I would have expected any gang of outlaws to head south once they were on the run. Out in the desert they would have a better chance of getting away. Once they got to the Mexican border, then they'd be clear and we would be able to do nothin'.'

Hilger pursed his lips into a tight, thoughtful line. 'That may be so,' he nodded. 'On the other hand, if I'm right about these men, this is only the first hold-up they mean to attempt. They'll strike again and again. This is a war against the railroad, not just a chance to get rich quickly and then get away from the scene. That being the case, they'd naturally head north, not only to throw you off the scent, but also to lose themselves in any one of a hundred cattle towns along the entire frontier. By now, they'll have made their plans to meet up again at some selected time and place.'

Crowden pushed the empty tin mug away from him with the flat of his hand and bent a long stare at Hilger. The latter could see the lawman's mind harden against him in spite of his own curiosity.

'If you are right, then there will be very little I can do to help you. Once they get outside my territory, it's up to some other sheriff.'

'I understand that, Sheriff. That's where we are a little more fortunate than you. Our organization is spread over more than a dozen states. We know no boundaries in our hunt against these men. We have more than five hundred agents throughout the length and breath of the country. I can pass on the description of Halloran to all of them within a radius of five hundred miles of Abilene and if these men are anywhere inside that circle, then sooner or later, they are going to give themselves away.'

'Then I wish you luck, Mister Hilger,' said Crowden heavily. There was a vague look of disbelief on his bluff features. 'And if you do find them, what then?'

Hilger shrugged. 'We shall hand them over to the law and let it deal with them. The charges will almost certainly be robbery with violence and murder. I think we all know the penalty for that.'

Crowden drummed softly on top of the desk with his fingers. 'You intend stayin' long in Abilene?'

'That depends. There may be other clues here which have been missed or overlooked. Abilene is, obviously, the best place from which to operate. I think I should get some results from the other Pinkerton agents scattered throughout the territory within the next week or so.'

Crowden smiled briefly, built himself a smoke, lit it and regarded Hilger curiously through the curling smoke. 'You're prepared to wait for two or three weeks?'

'I'm prepared to wait much longer than that, Sheriff, if it's necessary,' replied the other quietly.

7

The Time of the Outlaw

The towering thunderheads were boiling up over the eastern horizon as Ross Halloran rode the dusty trail which led north-east toward Dodge City. In spite of the dust, there was a pleasant fragrance to the air, the smell of sage, growing, in intensity as it always did in this part of the country just before any rain fell. It was now almost six months to the day since they had pulled that robbery of the express at Pecos Crossing. In all of that time, he had heard nothing of Dane or Blade. Like him, they appeared to have vanished completely from the scene. In each town that he came to, he bought and scanned each newspaper he could get his hands on, searching for any tiny piece of news which would give him an idea of what was happening in the State.

It had been four weeks since they had split up that he had come across the first of the wanted notices, nailed to a tall oak beside the trail. The poster had borne his picture and there was a reward of five hundred dollars for his capture, *dead or alive*.

It was the last phrase which had brought the slight chill to the pit of his stomach as he had paused to read the notice. For the first time, it came to him forcibly how precarious his position was so long as he remained within five hundred miles of Abilene. Since that time, he had grown a beard and his appearance had been sufficiently altered for him to be able to walk abroad in the many towns along his trail without too much fear of being recognized.

But those posters had told him that the hunt was on; that it was, indeed, being intensified. The Pinkerton Agency would not hesitate until they had found him, or the others, would not give in, even though it might take them years.

They operated slowly, taking their time, not hurrying things. They waited patiently for a man to make a mistake, knowing that sooner or later, he would do so and give himself away, and when it happened, they would be ready to step in and take him. The thought brought a tiny shiver to his mind as he spurred his mount, riding between tall cliffs of red sandstone that loomed high on either side of the trail. There was still some heat left in the sun, although the distant clouds were growing thicker now and a dark, black-purple haze blotted out details on the eastern horizon. Rain would come within the hour, he knew, and he would be wet before he reached Dodge.

Rubbing the beard on his chin, he thought ahead. Dodge City was the home of Wyatt Earp and Bat Masterton; both formidable lawmen and he knew that he would have to tread carefully while he was in town. On the other hand, the Pinkerton men would not think of looking for him where there were

147

such well known peace officers. They would be scouring the towns further to the north and east, which was one of the reasons why he had chosen Dodge as their rendezvous.

Pulling his mount off the trail near one of the wide bends, he gave it a chance to blow, wet his lips with water from his canteen. This territory was a thousand miles of nothing, he reflected idly. Some of it, where the great mountains rolled down from the horizons and thrust their huge shoulders against the trail seemed to be all tilted on edge, giving one the startling impression that he was riding on a continual slope. The rest of it was as flat as a grave, with the wind-blown dust lying inches thick over everything, most of it caustic alkali that burned a horse's hoofs and scorched a man's hands and face wherever it touched and clung. Waterless and absolutely sterile, it was a terrible country, that wanted nothing of men, that fought them with a hundred different deaths, from the rattler that struck without warning to a slow, lingering death from thirst and exhaustion. On the way he had passed several sun-bleached skeletons by the side of the trail and here and there, the rotting, warped boards of a Conestoga wagon, a grim relic of the days when men had first started out west over this tremendous country, seeking the promised land of California, so many weary miles to the West.

The powder-fine dust had formed a mask on his face from which his eyes looked out, red-rimmed and tender, his hide itching intolerably, his skin burning. He made himself a cigarette and thrust it unlit, between his lips, holding it there for several moments before striking a match and lighting it. The smoke burned his throat and lungs, but it gave him a chance to sit and think things out for a moment. If Dane and Blade made it all right, they should be in Dodge by now, or not far away. His lips curled a little in derisive humour as he visualized all of the Pinkerton agents rushing around the territory, trying to lay them by the heels. Soon, he promised himself, there would be another robbery, as daring as the last. When they did pull it off, he would see to it that it bore the unmistakable hallmark which had characterized the other. It was now becoming a matter of personal pride with him.

There was a fork-tongued flash of lightning low down to the east, racing across the heavens just above the horizon. The faint rumble of thunder that followed soon after, could just be heard. The clouds were dark now on the skyline and the black storm was sweeping nearer every moment. But he felt no hurry. The rain would come as a balm to his sun-scorched, dust-irritated skin. He sat straight in the saddle until he had finished his smoke, then leaned forward to pat the horse's neck, knowing how much the last few days' journey had taken out of the animal. It had carried him uncomplainingly over some of the worst, most rugged territory he had ever known.

A current of excitement flowed through his veins as he touched spurs to the horse's flanks once more, urging it back on to the trail. The terrain all about him appeared vacant as he rode in a wide sweep over the rough land, crossed the tracks of some large cattle herd which had obviously moved that way some time recently, then focused his eyes on the narrow ribbon of the trail where it ran as a pale grey scar over the barren ground.

There was another flicker of lightning, nearer this time and five minutes later the grey curtain of rain came sweeping down from the east and the first heavy drops of rain began to fall, sprouting in the dust around him, striking heavily at the brim of his hat. Within moments he was soaked to the skin, rode with his head lowered as the wind, which had risen with the approach of the storm, whipped at his face, the rain slashing viciously at him.

By the time he rode into Dodge, two hours later, the storm had passed over, and apart from an occasional blue-grey flicker of lightning off to the west, there was nothing to indicate that it had passed that way except for Ross's wet, steaming clothing and the muddy ground, the warmth of the early evening drawing the moisture from the soil in faint, miasmal mists that curled around him as he rode.

He crossed the plank bridge over a narrow creek, then rode on into the outskirts of Dodge. It was a typical frontier town, unlike Abilene in that it had not grown quite so large or sprawled out to the same extent. But it had obviously been patterned on the same design, had been thrown up by men in the same frame of mind as those who had built Abilene. He walked his mount along the wide main street, keeping his eyes alert, watching the boardwalks, letting his gaze pass over the buildings on either side of him, eyes missing nothing.

He located the hotel, the only two-storeyed

building along that particular stretch of the street, glanced ahead of him for a moment and then swung his mount, reining up in front of the hotel. Sliding from the saddle, he looped the reins over the low hitching rail and went inside. There was a small lobby and at the far end of it, the desk shrouded on either side by tall plants, he found the clerk.

'I'd like a room,' Ross said.

'Sure thing, mister,' nodded the other, getting to his feet. He laid down the newspaper he had been reading. 'Day, week or month?'

'Week,' Ross answered.

'That'll be twenty-five dollars,' said the other mildly. He pushed the book forward, offering Ross the pen.

For a moment, Ross looked at him in surprise. The other saw him hesitate, said quietly. 'You'd better make up your mind if you want the room, mister. We nearly always put the 'Full up' notice out before suppertime. And this is the only decent hotel in town.'

Ross sighed. He ought to have expected something like this, he told himself as he signed the register, using the name Thomas Kellin. Handing over the twenty-five dollars, he took the key, made his way up the stairs towards which the clerk pointed.

He found his room at the very end of the corridor at the top of the stairs, went inside and locked the door behind him. Taking off his jacket and shirt, unbuckling the heavy gunbelt from around his waist, he poured some water from the pitcher into the wide basin and washed himself, the mask of dried dust on his face and neck cracking audibly as the water softened it, peeling it away from his skin. He winced as the cold water touched his burnt flesh. On the trail, he had not really noticed the effect of the strong heat and sunlight on his skin. Now that he was able to wash the mask of dust off for the first time, he discovered just how hot it had really been.

Taking a fresh shirt from his saddle-roll, he slipped it on, buttoned it, then walked over to the window and glanced down into the street. It was almost suppertime now, the slack time, and there were few riders about, few men on the boardwalk. The first pale glimmers of yellow light were beginning to show in the windows of the buildings opposite and he clearly made out the tinny tinkling of a piano from the direction of one of the saloons.

He drank his fill from the water still left in the pitcher, glanced at his watch and saw that it still needed fifteen minutes to suppertime and made a cigarette. He had no real urge to smoke, but a cigarette could be utilized for other things too and he studied the street below him as he smoked. Overhead, the first stars were beginning to show in a purple heaven that had been washed free of dust by the passing storm.

A small bunch of men moved up from the far end of the street. From the window, he was able to see their dark shadows as they drifted through the gloom on the far plankwalk, their faces alternately lit and shadowed as they passed in front of the lamplit windows. The square-shaped silhouettes turned in at the saloon, thrusting open the batwing doors and moving inside.

Ross stayed where he was, his body pressed against the wall at the side of the window so that there was no danger of him being seen from the street while, at the same time, he was able to see all that went on below him. Five minutes later, there was the sound of a solitary rider drifting along the street from the eastern end of town. Ross kept a sharp look-out for the man, spotted him a moment later, riding slowly along the dusty river of the street. He stiffened a moment later as the rider drifted across the swathe of yellow light which spilled out into the street from above the doors of the saloon. The man ran a long look up and down the street as he rode by, and in that second that he passed through the light, Ross had been able to catch a quick glimpse of his face. It was all the time he needed to recognize the man. Blade had changed somewhat in the past six months. He no longer seemed to be as fresh looking as Ross remembered him; his features seemed more gaunt and lined than in those days only half a year before. The dark clothing that Blade wore was white-streaked with trail dust and as he rode, he kept one thumb hooked inside his gunbelt, close to the Colt slung low on his hip.

Ross watched the other closely until he had drifted out of sight, then turned away from the window. There was a faint feeling of relief in his mind at the fact that at least one of the others was safe and had managed to get there on time. Now it only needed Dane to ride in and they could start to make their plans. But they would have to be extra careful here in Dodge. Even though the chances were that the Pinkerton Agency had no agents here, neither Wyatt Earp nor Bat Masterton were men to be trifled with.

He buckled on the gunbelt once more,

checked his watch again, then cruised down the stairs and into the small dining-room set off the narrow lobby. Most of the tables were occupied, but he managed to find one set against the wall, so that he could sit facing the door. He ordered his meal and then sat back in the chair enjoying the opportunity to let all of his muscles loosen and relax. When the meal arrived he ate ravenously. It had been excellently cooked and the food acted as a stimulant to his jaded mind. He sipped the hot, black coffee slowly, savouring it, then sat back and built himself a cigarette. He had been tired when he had first arrived at the hotel. Now he was able to sit and think things out a little more clearly. Restlessness bubbled up inside him making him want to get to his feet and go out there into the night, find Blade and then go looking for Dane, to talk things over with the others, find out what had happened to them in the time that had passed since they had split up, discuss plans for their next robbery. But with a conscious mental effort, he forced the feeling away. Maybe it was the urges of a man who had to fight this war of vengeance against the North that was moving him like this. He knew, deep within himself, that the money had little to do with it. Undoubtedly, this was the only reason why Blade and Dane were in it with him. Once they figured they had enough money, they would pull out and leave him as Hank Morelle had done, would head for the Mexico border where they would be safe from the law.

Thinking of Hank, he wondered idly, speculatively, where the other was at that moment, whether he had made it safely or not. Whether he was still enjoying his life in Mexico, or perhaps yearning a little for the old days of excitement. Perhaps he had read of the hold-up of the express at Pecos Crossing and was wishing that he had stayed with them. Maybe not.

Ross finished his coffee, sat back in his chair and allowed his gaze to wander over the faces of the other folk in the dining room. Most of them looked like trail-herd men in from the surrounding ranches. But here and there were others who could be Pinkerton men, waiting patiently in every town along the frontier for them to strike once more. The organization would never give up.

Going out into the street, he led his horse along to the livery stable, watered it and then gave instructions to the groom. Coming out, he was on the point of making his way over to the saloon, when Blade's voice came to him from the dark shadows that lay thickly between two of the low-roofed buildings.

'Thought I recognized you as you went by. When did you get here?'

Ross paused for a moment, threw a quick glance up and down the street, then stepped quickly into the narrow alley. Blade's face was a pale grey blur in the shadows.

'I rode in this afternoon, about an hour ahead of you,' Ross said softly. 'I've got a room at the hotel, spotted you as you rode by.'

'I've put up at the lodging house a couple of hundred yards away. Any sign of Dane?'

'No. Could be that he hadn't got here yet. You have any trouble?'

'Not anythin' I couldn't handle,' replied the other easily. 'I came across some of those posters with your face on 'em. That why you grew the beard?'

'That's the main reason,' Ross agreed. 'Once Dane gets here, we'll talk things over. This is an uneasy town. Too many men around who could be railroad detectives or Pinkerton men. It's hard to be sure. We'll have to take things very slow and easy.'

'You could be right,' nodded the other

slowly. He searched for his tobacco and rolled a smoke blind in the darkness, struck and cupped the match to his face, blowing out a cloud of smoke in front of him. Momentarily, the orange glow from the match lit his lower face, almost touched his eyes. He drew deeply on the cigarette.

'There was nothin' in any of the news-papers about Dane, so I figure he's all right,' Ross said. 'But it's a long time and a long way from Abilene to Dodge. He may have had trouble gettin' here on time. Besides, a couple of days either way is nothin' in six months. I reckon we're lucky to be still around ourselves.'

Blade gave a brief nod. 'We'd better move real easy. This place is full of crooks and killers, hidin' out. So long as they don't bother the law none while they're here, they don't seem to be bothered in return. But all strangers ridin' into town are watched closely. I passed through here a couple of months ago and it's the same now as it was then. Every time I walked down the main street then I had the funny feelin' that somethin' was goin' to bust wide open at any minute and I'd be right in the middle of it all with lead flyin' from every goddamn direction.'

Ross said softly: 'If we do have to meet to talk, it'll be here after it's dark. Understood?'

'All right,' Blade nodded. 'How long are you goin' to wait for Dane? If he don't show up in the next few days – what then?'

'I guess we'll have to change our plans a little,' Ross said. He waited for a further moment then stepped to the end of the alley, peered off into the darkness that lay along this part of the main street, waited until he was sure there was no one around and then stepped out into the dusty thoroughfare and made his way towards the saloon.

Resting his elbows on the bar, he lifted a finger and when the barkeep came over, kept a tight hold on the bottle until the other nodded and moved away, leaving it with him. Now that Blade had got to Dodge safely, he felt the renewed current of interest running through him. From the far end of the bar, the bartender gave him a head-on glance, then looked down as he saw that Ross was watching him in return. He began to mop at the bar with the moist cloth he had with one end tucked into his belt. Ross poured himself a drink, tossed it down, felt it expand in his stomach in a warming haze. He poured another, drank this one more slowly.

As he drank, he began turning over in his mind all that he knew of Dodge. The railroad had come through a little over a year before, but the main stage line ran through the town and there was plenty of gold carried by the armoured stage coaches used by the banks for transporting currency and blocks of bullion from one place to another. It might be better, this time, to hold up one of the stages. Perhaps they would not get as much from it, but it would be a feather in their caps if they could do that and get away with it. So far as he knew, nobody had succeeded in holding up one of these specially armoured, well-guarded stages.

He filed that particular thought away in his mind. During the next few days, he would gain as much knowledge as he could about both the railroad and the stage-lines. There was a host of other questions he would need to find the answer to before he could finalize any plans. But he felt confident now. Things were working out the way he had planned them more than six months before.

The three men rode into Dodge from the west, arriving there shortly after full darkness was down. From the window of the hotel, Ross saw them come in, but for a long moment, his mind failed to connect them with Dane. Not until he saw Dane in the lead, did he experience a sudden feeling of unease. A second glance told him that the other was not a prisoner, that the men riding with him were not lawmen. Still, the uneasiness persisted as he went out of the hotel, walked over the street towards the saloon, making sure that Dane saw him as the three men lined up their mounts at the hitching rail and dismounted.

He noticed Dane flick a quick glance in his direction, saw from the faint look on the other's face that he had recognized him. Then he stepped into the saloon, letting the batwing doors swing back into place behind him. He walked across to the bar, stood leaning against it, watching the doors through the crystal mirror at the back of the room. There was a brief pause and then the doors were pushed open and Dane came in, flanked by the other two men. Ross studied their faces closely. He did not recognize either of them, but they appeared to be on friendly terms with Dane.

They came over to the bar, Dane standing close beside Ross, though seeming not to notice him.

Sliding the whiskey bottle towards the other, Ross said: 'Help yourself to this one. There's plenty in it.'

The barkeep, on the point of moving forward, stayed where he was, then turned his attention away from them, to the men at one of the tables. Dane said softly out of the corner of his mouth:

'I figured we might need some help, Ross, considerin' what happened the last time. These are a couple of boys who were in the same cavalry regiment as I was durin' the war. Bumped into 'em in Bitter Ridge. They're willin' to throw in with us if you give the word.'

'How much do they know of us?' Ross asked carefully. He felt a faint twinge of anger stirring inside him at what the other had done, then thrust it away. Maybe Dane was right. Only they would have to be sure these men could be trusted. The Pinkerton organization might have been clever enough to try to worm in some informers among their ranks.

'Not much,' Dane replied. He drank down his whiskey. 'I just told 'em that we might be able to pull a job or two around this part of the territory. You goin' to think about it, Ross?'

'I guess I've got to.' Ross lifted his weight slowly from the bar, let his keen glance slide over the two men who stood there. 'I reckon you know what will happen if you're wrong about 'em.'

'I'm not,' said the other slowly and with deep conviction. He nodded to the men: 'Charlie Monroe and Slim Mellor.'

Ross nodded briefly. 'My name is Kellin,' he said before Dane could put in a word. He saw the sudden look that flashed over the other's features, went on softly: 'Leastways that's the name I'm known by in Dodge. Anythin' else you may have heard, you forget.'

'Sure, sure,' muttered Monroe. 'We understand.'

'Good.' For a short space of time there was no more, talk. Then Ross went on quietly. 'Blade is in town, Dane. He rode in a couple of days or so ago, just after I got here. He's put up at the rooming-house on the edge of town, further along the street. I reckon it would be best if you three were to find a place at the other side of Dodge. Tomorrow night, ride out to the west. About three miles outside of town, the trail takes a sharp turn to the north. There's a stand of timber there. We can meet in there without attractin' any unwelcome attention.'

'We'll be there,' Dane said, nodding. He finished his drink, jerked his head towards the door and led the way out.

Ross Halloran felt worried and restless as he rode out of Dodge the next night. He felt that maybe he had staked a lot in trusting these two men that Dane had brought with him. Yet the other had seemed quite confident that they were men who could be trusted. If they had been with him in the Confederate Army, then the chances were that they, too, held a dislike for the Yankees and would be only too ready to continue the fight against them.

He had told Blade of their proposed meeting that morning, but had cautioned that it would be better if they rode separately out of the town, so that they would avoid causing any speculation. They had seen little of either Earp or Masterton, but he knew that both lawmen were around, somewhere in town and he did not relish the idea of having either of those men on his trail. Once or twice, he paused and peered into the growing darkness at his back, but could see no one else using the trail.

He came out finally on to more stony ground and the strike of his horse's hoofs on the hard earth was a steady ringing sound. Ahead of him, the thickening moon pushed itself up from behind the hills with a smooth, silent majesty, throwing a yellow light over the surrounding terrain, picking out the rocks and gullies in an etching of dark shadow. On either side of him, the flat desert lay quiet and lovely in the moonlight with little visible to break its wide and seemingly endless sweep off to the far horizons except for the occasional clump of sage and mesquite, with a few scattered patches of thorn and Spanish Sword.

As he rode, his thoughts went back in time, back to the days before the war when he had watched the moon come up on clear nights like this, when he had seen the stars shine down in their untold thousands forming a pale, shimmering glow in which it seemed that it was almost possible to hear the voice of God speaking out over the whole of Creation, so deep had been the silence of the desert. It was a pleasant reflection whenever he managed to reach back with his mind to those far-off days. But these memories were becoming more and more dimmed by succeeding events which tended to crowd them out, forcing them into a corner of his mind from which it was becoming increasingly difficult to extricate them.

His alertness increased as he realized that he had not got much further to go. He could dimly make out the dull patch of shadow where the timber lay on the lower slopes of the hill ahead of him. He rode over alkali sinks and ancient depressions which dotted the ground here and there, among a handful of stunted pines that lifted dark and gaunt against the moonlit sky. Their barren branches gave them a ghostly appearance in the night.

As he neared the meeting place, Ross's mind drew off for the last time and closed down on other things. What turn of events, or chain of events, had brought about this life he was now leading. The War? The Northern carpetbaggers who had ridden off the cattle from his home and forced him to kill two of them? The fact that the law now all seemed to be on the side of the victors who were steadily determined to destroy the South, to break the spirit of the Texans and grind it out altogether?

Half a year, he thought to himself, six months of running and hiding, of changing his identity, knowing that more than five hundred men had all combined in an all-out effort to hunt him and his companions down. How far away were these men now? Closing in on him, or just as far away as they had been that night six months before, when they had daringly held up the Abilene express and robbed them of almost seventy thousand dollars?

The world, for him, seemed to have turned into a complicated place, full of different turnings and trails which led into places whose existence he could never guess at until he arrived. Now he was too deeply involved in this to get himself clear. Maybe, if there was ever a chance in the future, when he had burned all of his hatred for the North out of his system, he might be able to do as Hank Morelle had done, ride south and get away from it all for good, spend the rest of his life in Mexico, not worrying who the next man on the street might be, whether a bullet might not come reaching out for him from the dark shadows of some street.

He somehow managed to free himself of these speculations; knowing that they had little bearing on his immediate future. What mattered now was those dark trees that lay a quarter of a mile ahead of him, and the plans would make for the next robbery. It required a moment for him to force his mind back to the present, but the urgency of the situation made him do it.

Slowly now, he rode forward along the winding trail which led off the main stage route. Against the dark velvet curtain of the night, the stars were clearly visible now, fading a little near the silver luminescence of the moon. There was a tiny, cool breeze drifting down from the summits of the hills, stirring the tall grass that grew on either side of the trail. Vaguely, he got the impression of other little, stray sounds off in the dimness of the hills where they pressed their rounded shoulders against the track.

Gripping the reins tightly, he entered the trees, both caution and interest blending with the growing excitement in his mind. As he rode, he watched the margins of the timber, remembering those two men who had ridden into Dodge with Dane, still not quite trusting them, even though the other had vouched for them. It was unlikely that Dane would have brought them there if he had not been absolutely certain of their loyalty, but Ross was not the kind of man to take any unnecessary chances, particularly where his own neck was concerned. It needed only one mistake, and they were finished. The Pinkerton men were just waiting for that fatal slip, just waiting to move in once they had sufficient evidence.

He moved on through the loose screen of first-growth pines, deeper into the forest. Wheeling in, he came on the tangled root system of a fallen tree and moving around it, caught the smell of cigarette smoke, a second before he sighted the four men standing in the shadows.

8

Train Wreck

'Earp was out with a posse this afternoon,' Dane said, as Ross slid from the saddle and walked towards the waiting group. 'We were just out of town when we spotted him.'

'You reckon he may have got word from the Pinkerton Agency about us?' Blade asked. He stood with his back against one of the trees, a tall dark shadow.

'I doubt it.' Ross shook his head. 'Nobody

knows we're here. I figure that if Earp was after us, he's just guessin'. Anyway, we'll be away from here by this time tomorrow.'

'You figured out another plan?' It was one of the men who had ridden in with Dane who spoke up from the dimness.

'Could be.' Ross tightened his lips a little, flicked a quick glance at Dane. 'Where do you two men fit in? You ready to throw in your lot with us, even if it means having half a thousand men on your tail once we pull another job?'

Both men nodded. 'Dane said you was one of the best planners in the business,' murmured Monroe. 'We read about that hold-up of the express at Pecos Crossing. You took that train easily enough.'

'Maybe so. But they weren't expectin' it then. They know that sooner or later, we're goin' to strike again. They'll have been expectin' us to lie low for a while until that last affair blew over. Things are goin' to get more difficult and dangerous as time goes on. And believe me, you'll both be marked men if you throw in with us.'

Mellor shrugged. 'We've been on the run since the war finished. They haven't forgotten that we were beaten. They spit on us and treat us like dirt. They've taken away our homesteads, made us go without food, driven off our cattle. There are new taxes bein' imposed every day, everythin' designed to force us out of business or grind us into the dirt.'

'All right.' Ross led his horse over to the others. 'Let's get down to business. I've been learnin' plenty while I've been in Dodge. The railroad brings in the gold in an armoured van, always at the end of the train and guarded by at least three men. Since our last hold-up they've got into the custom of telegraphing ahead from the small way stations if the train is to stop there. I suspect that they may use a code, so we can't do the same thing ourselves.'

'So they just run on through if red signals are set to stop 'em,' Blade said tightly.

'That's right. So we have to use some other way of stoppin' the train just where we want it to stop.'

'How do you figure doin' that?' asked Monroe. He lit a cigarette, blew the smoke into the air.

'Dynamite,' Ross said softly.

'You mean blow up the train?' asked Dane incredulously.

'Why not?' put in Blade with a harsh laugh. 'We did worse things durin' the war and—'

'But that *was* war,' Dane said hollowly. 'Blowin' up a train and killin' innocent people is a different thing. We'd really have the Pinkerton men after us then.'

'No need to blow up the train,' Ross interrupted calmly. 'My idea is to destroy the track just before the train is due. There's a sharp bend in the track fifteen miles east of here where the rails run through a steep canyon. It's the ideal place for a job like this.'

'When do we do it?' inquired Dane tautly. The tip of his cigarette glowed redly in the dimness as he drew deeply on it.

'Tomorrow. I've got the dynamite stashed away in a small hut just over the hill. Ain't no need for any of us to go back into Dodge.'

The others were silent at that for a moment, then Blade said slowly: 'I guess that's the best way, Ross.' His words held a significant meaning and Ross knew that the other was shrewd enough to have understood the reason for this. Just in case either of the two men with Dane was working for the Pinkerton Agency, this would prevent them from giving away the information they had just learned to anyone in Dodge. By the time they were able to do so, it would be too late, the robbery would have taken place and they would both have been implicated in it.

The first steely palings of dawn found the bunch of men on the far side of the range of hills, coveting ground at a consuming gait. In front of them the pinched-down mountains moved back from the trail and they were riding through low mounds where in places, the bare rocks thrust themselves out of the grass and vegetation. They splashed through a swift-running torrent that spilled down the hillside and then on through tall grass which deadened the sound of their horses.

The trail began its gradual descent just as the sun was lifting clear of the eastern horizon, snaking down into the red fir lowlands which divided the hills from the plains. By mid-morning, they were among the lower slopes and two hours before high noon, they came on the small clearing in which stood the wooden hut, its roof twisted and warped by the strong sun, one of the walls bulging outward as if punched from the inside by a mighty fist.

'This the place?' Blade asked, leaning forward in his saddle and shading his eyes from the sunlight.

'This is it,' Ross answered. He led the way into the stony clearing in front of the hut, dismounted, and tied the reins to the lop-sided hitch rail. There was little furniture inside the hut. It had evidently been built by one of the prospectors panning for gold in the swift-running streams that flowed down through the trees on the rocky slope. But the place had been abandoned long before the war even and Ross doubted if anyone ever came this way now. It had seemed the ideal place in which to hide the explosive.

The box of dynamite was still in one corner where he had left it and there was no evidence that anyone had been there since himself. 'We've got an hour before we have to pull out,' he told the others. 'There are some vittles in the bag yonder. We'd better eat while we have the chance.'

While the others lit a fire to cook the food, he went outside with Blade. Lighting a cigarette, he stared off into the greenness that lay all about them. He was silent for a long moment and it was Blade who spoke first, breaking the tensed, uneasy silence.

'You're still not sure about those two hombres, are you?'

Ross stared down at his cigarette for a moment, lips tight, then shrugged. 'Until I am sure, I figured it would be best to have them stay with us all the way. Once we've finished this job, I may be able to tell for sure whether they're all they say they are.'

Blade sighed. 'About four months ago,' he said softly, 'I went back into Abilene. Just curiosity, I reckon.'

Ross's eyes widened. 'Is that so, Blade? I didn't know. You hear anythin'?'

'There was a man there called Hilger. He'd taken over the inquiries about the hold-up.'

'A Pinkerton man?'

'One of their best, they reckon. He's directing the organization there. I tried to learn all I could about him. He's one of the most important men in the organization. Whatever happens, it would be unwise to underestimate him.'

'I saw a mention of him in one of the news-papers. But until now, he's been nothin' more than a name.'

'He's got more than a score of men workin' for him. Some travel on the trains in the state, keepin' their eyes open. He was the one who arranged for your picture to be put up on those wanted posters.'

'But this isn't Abilene, Blade. This is Dodge territory. Earp and Masterton are in control here and I get the feelin' that when a Southerner is concerned, that control is pretty slender. Most of the folk here are sympathizers of the Southern cause, even though the war has been over for some time. If Hilger tried to move in here, he'd have to feel his way around pretty slowly. Earp doesn't like anybody homin' in on his territory.'

'That won't stop Earp from comin' after us when we pull this job,' Blade said harshly. 'He's a fast man with a gun. That goes for Bat Masterton too. They've both sworn to keep the peace in Dodge and they'll do it, whether we're Southerners or not.'

'They'll have to catch us first and this country is some of the best for men on the run.' He dropped the butt of his cigarette to the ground and heeled it into the dirt. 'Let's get somethin' to eat. Not much time left and we'll have to place that explosive in just the right place. It's tricky stuff to handle at the best of times.'

Fifty minutes later, they rode out of the clearing, the explosive distributed among them, tied securely to their saddle-bags. Neither of the two men had questioned his decision not to ride back into Dodge and as they rode, it seemed more and more that they were genuine and his original suspicions had been ill-founded. But he still refused to relax his vigilance. The muscles about Ross's jaw-line knotted and he settled himself squarely in leather. His mind forgot everything but the job in hand, his thoughts roving ahead.

Zig-zagging down a steep slope, covered with flint and loose shale, they came out of the trees a quarter of a mile above the canyon. Down below them in the early afternoon sunlight, the gleaming rails curved away into the canyon and then twisted south sharply, converging into a point in the far distance. Ross reined up and pointed.

'There's the canyon,' he said quietly. 'We plant the explosive just inside and near the southern end. Once the dynamite goes off, it'll not only tear up the track but it ought to bring the canyon walls down on it, blocking, it altogether. That way, they don't have a chance of drivin' on into Dodge and givin' warning of what's happened. Somebody will have to go in on foot and that should give us plenty of time to make a getaway.'

They led their horses down into one of the dense thorn thickets that grew just above the rim of the canyon, made them fast there, then took out the dynamite and the lengths of fuse and carried them carefully down the slope.

'I've used this stuff before,' Monroe said, standing beside the track and throwing a speculative glance up at the steep-sided rock walls. 'I can put it just where it will have the most effect.'

Ross hesitated for the barest fraction of a second and then nodded slowly. 'All right, Monroe. But make sure that you do it properly. We can't afford any mistakes.'

With a nod, the other moved along the track, glanced in both directions, then said: 'We'll put one charge here. Better dig a hole for the dynamite, then cover it with rocks. That'll increase the effect of the blast.'

Ten minutes later, a hole had been scooped from the rocky earth beneath the rails and half of the dynamite placed inside it, the long fuse snaking out of the hole.

'How will I know when to light the fuses?' Monroe asked, glancing up at Ross.

The other paused, then jerked a thumb towards the rim of the canyon. 'I'll be up there,' he said shortly. 'As soon as you see me give the signal, light them both and then get the hell out of there.' He let his gaze roam over the rocky wall of the canyon nearby, then indicated the narrow trail cut in the side. 'There's your best way out. If you try to run along the canyon floor you'll never make it. Head up there and once you get to the top, move back in that direction. That way, you ought to be out of the way of flyin' rock.'

Monroe nodded in understanding, began to place several large rocks on top of the hole containing the explosive. When he had finished, there was no sign of it apart from the fuse leading down into it. Moving a few yards back along the track, he repeated the procedure. Finally, he was satisfied.

'You're sure you know exactly what to do?' Ross asked.

'No need to worry none,' muttered the other. 'I've handled this stuff before like I said.'

Ross eyed him for a long moment, then turned away and signalled to the others to move out. He consulted his watch. There were less than ten minutes left before the train was scheduled to pass through the canyon. By the time they had reached the top of the canyon, there was a faint cloud of black smoke just visible on the far horizon and a few moments later, the mournful wail of the engine's whistle came to them across the plain.

'There she is,' said Dane excitedly. He pointed. 'Right on schedule.'

Ross edged closer to the rim of the canyon. From where he stood, he could look down and see Monroe standing close to where the first charge of dynamite had been laid. The other had built and lit himself a cigarette and Ross guessed that he had done this to light the fuses. There was a stiff breeze blowing along the canyon, funnelled through the rocky walls and a match was too uncertain in such conditions.

Monroe was watching him closely, waiting for his signal. Ross gave a faint, mirthless grin. The tight sense of excitement was piling up inside him again, as it had on that previous occasion when he had stood on the observation car of the Abilene express, waiting for the train to slow.

The train came on over the plain and it was possible now to make out the shape of the locomotive with the plume of black smoke standing out behind it, streaming back over the coaches. He judged it was less than two miles distant. Everything would have to be timed down to the last second now and none of the men in the group realized that more than he did. If the explosive went off too soon, there would be a chance for the engineer to stop the train and then put the locomotive into reverse and the guards would have ample warning of what was going on. If the dynamite exploded too late, the entire train would be inside that canyon by the time it went off and countless innocent people would be killed, which was the last thing that Ross wanted.

He waited with a growing impatience as the train continued its apparently snail-like approach. The whistle sounded again, possibly to warn the passengers that they were approaching the canyon. Ross fixed his eyes on a short wooden post which had been hammered into the ground near the track about two hundred yards before the trail began its sharp turn. He reckoned that once the locomotive reached that post, he could give the signal.

Beside him, Blade watched the train come closer, smoke belching from the funnel. The metal gleamed brilliantly in the lancing sunlight, the roar of the pistons growing louder with every passing second. Then he switched his glance swiftly to Ross's face. What in tarnation was the other waitin' for now? he wondered fiercely. If he didn't give the signal soon, the train would be through the canyon and out at the other side before the long fuses burned through.

Then, abruptly, Ross raised his right hand so that Monroe could see it clearly, held in there for a moment; then brought it down sharply. At the same moment, Monroe bent, touched the end of his cigarette to the fuse, waited for a few seconds to make sure that it was burning, then ran to the second length of fuse, repeated the procedure, hesitated for a second longer, then ran for the narrow track that wound up the side of the canyon. Down there, owing to the sharp bend in the track, he was hidden from anyone on board the train.

Ross watched intently as the other scrambled up the steep slope, clawing his way upward, legs and arms thrusting him up. Behind him, the fuses spluttered and burned, tiny wisps of smoke coming from them as the flame licked its way along the length of black powder, eating towards the dynamite buried in the holes beneath the rails.

Monroe heaved himself over the top of the canyon rim, lay panting for a moment from his exertions, then got to his feet, keeping his head low and ran to where Blade and Ross were waiting. The other two men were on the far side of the canyon, crouched down behind the huge boulders there, protected by them from any falling rock.

'Everythin' all right?' Ross asked tightly as Monroe threw himself down beside them.

The other nodded tersely. 'I figured you were never goin' to give the signal,' he muttered jerkily. 'I only hope you didn't hold off until too late.'

'We'll soon see,' was all Ross said. He held his breath as the train came thundering along the track, heading for the canyon. Perhaps he had held off too long. How slowly did that goddamned fuse burn? Maybe he had not allowed for it, maybe–

The thunderous detonations came so close together that they might have been a single explosion. With a deafening roar, the dynamite exploded, sending huge boulders and twisted pieces of metal geysering high into the air. The booming echoes were still chasing themselves along the canyon when the vast, cavernous rumbling reached their numbed ears as the walls of the canyon slid down into the opening and the rocks avalanched on to the torn and twisted section of track.

Several boulders bounced off the rocky ground close to their prone bodies as they thrust themselves hard against the dirt. Dust and fumes bit at their nostrils and stung their eyes and throats. For several seconds, Ross lay there, dazed, scarcely able to think properly. Then, with an effort, he thrust himself to his feet, stood up groggily, peering about him through the cloud of dust that obscured his vision. Beside him, Blade and Monroe staggered to their feet. The tremendous, concussive blast had been far greater than any of them had anticipated.

Grabbing Monroe by the arm, he propelled him forwards, over the rocks which now lay strewn in their path. Wiping a hand over his sweating face, Ross pulled the linen duster up around his nose and mouth, running forward as quickly as he dared, jerking his gun from its holster as he ran. Vaguely, he was aware of the other two following him, now having recovered from the numbing blast.

Through the thinning haze of dust, Ross saw that the train was slowing to a halt, sparks flying redly from beneath the wheels as the engineer applied the brakes frenziedly. For a moment, it seemed impossible that he would be able to stop the train in time. Then, with a final squeal of metal on metal, the engine came to rest within ten feet of the pile of rocks which had crashed down into the canyon, obliterating the track altogether.

Swiftly, Blade swung himself up into the locomotive. The engineer turned as he reached the level of the platform, swung the heavy shovel which he had snatched up at the other's head. The fireman, on the other side, dropped down to the side of the track and began running along the train to warn the conductor.

Savagely, Blade lunged forward, butting the engineer in the stomach with his lowered head. There was a sudden agonized whoosh as the other's breath gasped from between parted lips and he staggered back against the firebox with a scream of agony, the shovel falling from his hands as the hot metal burned his back. Without pausing, Blade lifted his gun, holding it by the barrel and swung it in a short arc against the engineer's temple. Without any further cry, he fell forward, collapsing at the other's feet. There was the shrill hiss of escaping steam, but Blade did not pause to examine this. Leaping down from the cab of the locomotive, he moved back along the train. Dane and Mellor were already moving through the coaches, taking the valuables from the passengers.

There was little resistance under the menacing guns carried by the outlaws. Anyone who attempted to fight was knocked down by a brutal blow from the butt of a revolver.

While this was taking place, Ross and Monroe had reached the express car at the rear of the train. Crouching down near the door, Ross yelled: 'All right, open up in there! You've got exactly one minute before we start shootin'.'

There was no answer from inside. Then, without warning, the door of the coach nearby was flung open and two men came out on to the platform. Both had guns in their hands and opened up at once. A slug ricocheted off the metal of the car within an inch of Ross's head as he pulled himself back, bringing up his own gun. He had hoped that they might be able to do without shooting, but there was no place for such chivalry here. He snapped off a shot that hit one of the men in the shoulder, spinning him around, pitching him forwards over the low rail, the gun dropping from his hand. The second man went down on one knee, continued to fire, loosing off shot after shot. At the same time, the metal door of the express car slid open a couple of inches and the barrel of a rifle poked through just beside Monroe's head.

With a sudden yell, he reached up, caught

hold of the rifle barrel, jerked it savagely to one side, sliding the door back on its grooved runners, then heaved. There was a wild cry of terror from inside and the next moment, the conductor came sailing out of the car, hitting the ground in a crumpled heap. He lay quite still, either killed or knocked unconscious by the force of the impact.

'Get inside,' Ross ordered sharply. 'I'll take care of these two guards.'

Without hesitation, Monroe caught hold of the bottom of the opening, pulled himself inside. There was the sound of a short, sharp scuffle, then silence.

'You all right, Monroe?' Ross called.

'Sure. There was a messenger inside. He won't give us any more trouble.'

'Good. See what you can find in there. If my information was right, there should be enough to make this worthwhile.' Twisting from the waist, he saw the weaving pattern of the second man on the nearby observation platform moving clear of the man slumped near the rail. The guard's hand did not lift, but merely twisted from the wrist as he sought to bring the gun to bear on Ross. The other's gaze was bright with triumph. His gun was free and lining up on Ross's body. Then Ross moved. The gun seemed to move in his hand of its own accord, lining up on the other's chest even as he snapped down the barrel a little and squeezed the trigger. The guard's tipped barrel sagged drunkenly downward and exploded thunderously, the bullet ploughing into the earth a couple of feet from where Ross was standing, his back pressed against the metal of the express car. The stink of burnt powder was sharp in Ross's nostrils and through the blue haze of smoke he saw the other lurch, then fall forward, his body overbalancing over the rail and crashing on to the track between the two coaches.

Ross lingered long enough to ensure that the other was dead and there was no further menace from the coach, then pulled himself up into the car. Monroe was squatting on the floor beside two large cases. Both had steel bands around them, padlocked with a heavy lock.

Thrusting the other to one side, Ross aimed his gun at the lock and pulled the trigger. The sound of the two gunshots was loud in the confined space of the car, almost deafening them, but the locks had been completely shattered, the metal bands sprung open.

'Empty them into the sacks,' Ross ordered. 'I'll watch the door just in case there are any other guards on board the train.'

He could hear the faint screams of some of the women passengers inside the train as the others went through the coaches, taking everything they could find. It was unlikely that they would get anything as important as the gold in the express car, but it would keep the others occupied and lessen the chance of anybody deciding to be a hero.

Five minutes later, Monroe was beside him, dragging the heavy sacks over the floor of the car.

'That the lot?' Ross asked.

The other nodded quickly. 'Nothing but mail in those other sacks,' he said, jerking a thumb towards the pile in the corner.

'Then let's get out of here.' Ross dropped lightly to the ground, lifted down the heavy sacks as the other passed them out to him. The conductor moaned a little, tried to push himself to his feet, then fell back, the effort too much for him.

'Do we finish him off?' Monroe asked, his voice utterly emotionless.

Ross shook his head. 'He can't do anythin',' he said sharply. Lifting his gun, he fired three quick shots into the air.

Two hours later, riding by a circuitous route, they were back in the small prospector's shack deep in the timber. Soberly, Ross divided the amount they had taken. Less than that which they had got from their first hold-up, it was still a goodly sum.

Placing his share in one of the wheat sacks, Dane said: 'There's goin' to be all hell let loose around here as soon as somebody from that train gets into Dodge, Ross. Do we split up here and stay low like we did before?'

Ross shook his head without hesitation. 'No. That's what they'll be expectin' us to do after the last time. My guess is they won't be able to follow our trail far. The rocks will have blotted it out half a mile from the canyon. We'll shack up here for a couple of days and then strike again before they're expectin' any more trouble.'

'You're goin' to hit the railroad again inside two days?' There was a note of incredulity in Monroe's voice. He stared at the other, his mouth hanging slackly open. 'But that's crazy!'

'Not the railroad,' Ross said quietly, almost as though he had not heard the other's final outburst. 'The stage road runs through the

191

hills north of here and we're goin' to take the armoured stage that carries most of the bullion.'

Blade whistled thinly through his teeth. 'Now that's a mighty tall order, even for us,' he said. 'They have a posse ridin' with that stage, a dozen men or more. It won't be as easy as holding up the train.'

With a nod, Ross tied the neck of the sack in front of him, carried it to one corner and placed it down carefully. 'Could be that you're right at that,' he agreed. 'But suppose,' he said eventually, speaking slowly because he was simultaneously forming an idea and a sentence, 'suppose we was to start a ruckus a little way off the trail, draw off most of the posse. Could give two of us a chance to sneak up on the stage and hit the others before they knew we was there.'

Blade continued to look dubious, but said nothing as he shifted his body into a more comfortable position.

9

Guntrail

The hotel bed had been hard and lumpy and Kirby Hilger had slept badly during the night. As a result, he felt tired and irritable as he dressed, then made his way down into the dining room. Abilene had been bad compared with the cities of the East, but Dodge City was a hundred times worse. The heat and the flies in the dining room were troublesome and the food was cool and badly cooked. He washed it down with the hot coffee, then got to his feet and went out into the dusty street. The stage was standing in front of the depot taking on the passengers who were heading back east.

He saw the strongbox being tossed high on to the driver's seat and a moment later, the man riding shotgun came out of the stage depot and swung himself easily up beside the grey-whiskered driver. Musingly, Hilger stood against the wooden rail of the boardwalk as the driver brought the long whip snaking down on to the backs of the horses, uttering a shrill yell. There was the grind of wheels in the dust and the stage swung out and away from the depot and headed along the street, throwing up a grey cloud of dust behind it, dust which settled only slowly in the still air.

It had been late the previous night when he had arrived in Dodge City on that same stage. The journey had been slow and uncomfortable, the stage oppressively hot, but whenever they had let down the windows to ease the terrible heat, the dust had come in, making life even more unbearable than before. He continued to stare along the street long after the stage had vanished around the corner, leaving only the slowly-settling dust in its wake. He felt weary inside, and it was a tiredness that came from something more than the long journey and the little sleep he had had during the night.

For six months he had been hoping that one of the men working for him would come up with something that would give him a clue as to the whereabouts of those outlaws who had held up the Abilene train and got away with all of that gold. But the days had lengthened into weeks and then into months and still there had been nothing. He had begun to despair of ever finding anything that would give him a lead.

Then had come word of the attack on the train outside Dodge City. There had been nothing conclusive to link this attack with that near Abilene; yet in his mind there was that feel which he had learned, from past experience, never to ignore. He felt certain that the hold-ups had been the work of the same men, even though this time the passengers had spoken of five men holding up the Dodge City train.

Whoever they were, they had kept out of sight during the six months that had just passed. And the precision with which they had worked, indicated that the man who led them was no fool. Kirby Hilger never underestimated any outlaw. These men lived by their wits and by striking suddenly and without warning. But invariably they planned their hold-ups well, vanishing into the wilderness in this territory, leaving little trace.

The hell of it was that he had sworn to capture the men responsible. The task had been thrust on him by Headquarters in Missouri and when he had first ridden into Abilene, he had been certain that he could crack this case wide open in a very little time. But even though this outlaw band had done exactly as he had anticipated, had held up another train, he was still no closer to capturing them than he had been six months before.

Jerking his thoughts back to the present, he pulled himself together, continued on his way to the sheriff's office. Knocking loudly on the door, he went inside. He recognized the two men in the office immediately. From what he had heard of Wyatt Earp and Bat Masterton, he was not sure whether he liked them, or their methods. Very often, it seemed, they were as much on the side of outlawry as on the side of law and order. Yet, it was true, as he was forced to admit, that these two men had brought an uneasy kind of peace to this frontier hell-town, a law and order which had been noticeably lacking before they had arrived on the scene.

Wyatt Earp rose slowly to his feet, extended his hand to the other. 'You'll be Kirby Hilger,' he said in a slow drawl. 'Saw you arrive on the stage last night.'

Hilger nodded. Bat Masterton gave him a brief nod of acknowledgment, remained standing near the window, seemingly absorbed in watching the scene in the dusty street outside, rather than showing any interest in what was happening in the office.

Hilger felt a faint stirring of anger, but kept it under tight control. However much he might dislike the attitude of these two men, he needed their help if he was to get anywhere on this case. He had been acutely aware ever since he had arrived in the town that here his reputation counted for very little, that these men probably disliked him as much as he did them.

'Won't you take the weight off your feet, Hilger?' Wyatt nodded towards the chair in front of the desk. 'I gather you have somethin' on your mind. Is it to do with the train hold-up?'

Hilger nodded. 'There was a similar robbery six months ago near Abilene.'

'And you reckon the same gang did this one?' Masterton spoke from the window, his tone shrewd.

'I'm sure they did. They both have the same characteristics as if they were planned by the same man. In my business you get to recognize the way in which men work.'

Earp raised his brows a little. 'Just what is your business, Mister Hilger?'

'I work for the Pinkerton Agency. My job is to bring these outlaws to book. It could be that they still have most of the gold with them. If they have, it belongs to the banks.'

Earp was silent for a moment, turning that over in his mind. From the window, Masterton said harshly: 'Those outlaws, even if they are the same ones you're lookin' for, will be a hundred miles away by now. We rode out with a posse to the place where the track had been blown up, but we lost their trail within half an hour. It led up into the rocks and not even an Apache could have followed it through that kind of country. They won't be fool enough to stay in this territory.'

'But that's where I'm sure you're wrong,' Hilger persisted. 'I've been searching through the records. I know as much about this man, Ross Halloran, as he does about himself.'

Wyatt Earp knitted his brows into a straight line. He regarded the other closely for a long moment. 'What do you know of him?'

'He's either a fool or very sure of himself. I've known many men like him and none of them have used their real names as he did in Abilene.'

'How can you be so sure it is his name?' Masterton asked, turning.

'I traced his record all the way back. He

joined the Confederate Army six months after the outbreak of war, fought in the Wilderness until the peace was signed at Appamattox Courthouse. When he arrived back home in Texas, he killed two men who rustled off some of their cattle under the guise of taking the animals to check on the so-called Texas fever.' Hilger shrugged. 'Perhaps he was in the right, defending his own place like that, but the law thought otherwise. He fled before the local sheriff could take him and from that point on, he must have thrown in his lot with a band of outlaws, finally taking over command.'

'And how can we help you in this matter?'

'I'm sure that these men are still in the territory. They'll strike again, and soon. I'm sure they won't lie low for another six months before attacking again. I'm equally certain they won't attack the railroad this time.'

'If they try to hold up the bank in Dodge they're fools,' Bat Masterton said positively. 'We'll empty their saddles before they can ride the length of the main street.'

'I don't doubt it,' Hilger acknowledged. 'But there is still the armoured stage.'

'What's on your mind?' asked Earp darkly. 'You reckon they'll try for it?'

Hilger looked at the lawman with some care. It was plain that the other was convinced Halloran and his bunch were now nowhere in his territory and he was reluctant to believe otherwise. He nodded his head in affirmation. 'I'm damned sure he will. He has four men with him now. I've no idea who they are, but judging from what happened a couple of days ago, they know how to handle guns and they're mighty dangerous.'

There was a bright glint in Wyatt Earp's eyes as he surveyed Hilger closely. He took time over his reply. 'If you want to know what I think, Hilger, these *hombres* are just fast gunslingers from down south, quick on the draw maybe and with plenty of grit.'

'He's a real hell-raiser, I don't doubt, but if you agree to play things my way, I reckon we can get him. Don't forget there's a reward of fifty thousand dollars on his head alone, put up by my organization. Ten thousand for each of the others riding with him.'

'A lawman don't get the chance to collect any rewards for outlaws and killers,' Earp reminded him. 'Still, I'm willin' to listen to this plan of yours.' He settled himself deeper in his chair, legs thrust out straight in front of him, his eyes narrowed down to mere slits.

Hilger turned his head to look at Bat Masterton as the other moved around from the window and stood behind the desk beside Wyatt Earp. There was a faint look of derision on the other's face but he made no comment, waiting for Hilger to speak.

'Halloran is around here some place. These hills are twenty miles long and fifteen miles wide and there are plenty of places in there where this bunch can hide until they're ready to make another move. By now, they'll know every stop the trains and that stage make within fifty miles of here. They can hit the stage anywhere between Butte Point and here.'

'Mister Hilger,' said Bat Masterton. 'Please give us credit for some sense. We know that this stage is a temptation for any band of outlaws. That is why we have a posse ridin' with it every time it makes a trip carryin' gold. You've just said yourself that there are only five men in this gang. How do you figure they can overcome a dozen armed and seasoned gunfighters?'

'I'm coming to that.' Hilger moved his body into a more comfortable position. 'They'll know about this posse so they'll have figured out some way of drawing it off. Some kind of disturbance a little way off the trail. That would split your posse. They may even use dynamite again, although I doubt it, but it's a possibility you can't afford to overlook.'

He saw the growing look of indecision in the lawman's eyes. Pressing home his advantage, he went on quickly. 'My plan is this. I can travel on that stage from Butte Point, ready for any trouble from that end. If you would handle it with the posse from the other end, I'm convinced we could take the whole bunch.'

'You're willin' to risk your life?' Earp asked. There was still no emotion in his voice. 'If anythin' should go wrong with this plan, you'd be the first to get it.'

'I realize that,' Hilger muttered. 'But I've been looking for this man for six months now. He's made a laughing stock of me and of the organization I work for. I intend to get him if it's the last thing I do.'

'From what I've heard about him,' murmured Bat Masterton, 'it could well be.'

'Can I count on your co-operation, gentlemen?' Hilger asked harshly. He let his gaze wander from one man to the other. He was well aware that his personal problems made little impression on either of these men.

'Very well,' nodded Earp at length. 'I'll fix

somethin'. The next stage that carries gold is due to leave Butte Point the day after tomorrow. If you really want to go through with this, I suggest that you be on it.'

The stage came rattling around the corner of the square in Butte Point shortly after the first grey streaks of dawn appeared over the low range of hills to the east. It slewed to a standstill in front of the stage depot in a cloud of grey dust kicked up by the plunging feet of the horses in the traces. The bearded oldster in the driver's seat clambered down into the street, paused for a couple of minutes to glance about him, then brushed the back of his sleeve over his dust-smeared features before pulling a flat bottle of liquor from his hip pocket and taking a quick swallow. His lips twisted into a faint grimace as he stared down at the bottle for a moment, before he thrust it back and stumped up the steps into the depot.

Kirby Hilger watched him go inside, then followed on the other's heels into the long, low-roofed building. He walked over to the register desk that stood at one end and deposited his bag on the floor in front of it, straightening up and peering through the iron grille at the sleepy-eyed clerk behind the desk. The other glanced through at him, then lifted his brows slightly.

Pulling out a wad of bills, Hilger said: 'What's the fare into Dodge from here?'

'The fare is twenty-five dollars, mister,' said the other harshly, 'but not by the stage you see outside.'

'Why not?' Hilger asked thinly. 'I've got the money here and from what I've heard it's the only stage pulling out in that direction this morning. If I wait until the afternoon I shall be too late arriving in Dodge City.'

The other's lips drew back in a faint grin. 'Mister, you must be a stranger in this part of the territory. But that happens to be the special stage that runs to Dodge. No passengers are allowed on board.'

'That may well be so, but I don't happen to be any passenger,' Hilger said tightly. He took out his card, slid it through the iron grille. 'As you'll see from that I happen to be working for the Pinkerton Agency. It's vitally important that I get into Dodge. If you want any further confirmation of this, I suggest that you wire ahead to Wyatt Earp about me. He'll confirm who I am and that I can travel on this stage.'

At the mention of Marshal Earp's name, the other's attitude changed at once, and any doubts he may still have had were dispelled by the card which Hilger had handed him. He pushed it back through the bars, took the fare which Hilger gave to him. Shrugging his thin, sloping shoulders, he said: 'If that's the way you want it, Mister Hilger. The stage leaves in fifteen minutes. It's a fast, hard run with a change of horses around one o'clock. You'll get into Dodge at ten o'clock tonight, all bein' well.'

'You expectin' trouble then?'

The other shrugged once more. 'No way of tellin', Mister. The train was derailed and held up a couple of days ago. They do say that the Halloran gang is still in the territory. If they are, then they may make a try for this stage.' He took a book out from under the desk. 'I'll have to have your name here, Mister Hilger. Just for the Company's records, you understand.'

Hilger wrote his name in the book, then closed it and slid it back beneath the grille. The clerk's eyes narrowed a little as he let his gaze wander over Hilger's clothing. 'You don't seem to be packin' a gun, mister,' he said quietly. 'That might be a mistake with this stage.'

'I understood that a posse travelled with us,' Hilger said.

'That's so. But they don't join up with you until you get to the way station. You travel through some pretty rough country before then.' There was an uneasy smile on the other's face that did not touch his eyes, merely curling the corners of his mouth.

Hilger nodded. 'Thanks for the warning anyway,' he said, picking up his bag, 'but I do happen to carry a pistol with me. A small one, but just as deadly as a Colt, I assure you.'

He knew that the other's eyes were still on him as he walked towards the door, but did not turn to glance back. He waited outside on the boardwalk until the driver emerged from the depot. There was a slight heat in the air even at that early hour of the morning and he knew inwardly that it was going to be another highly uncomfortable ride for him. He thought of the last stage ride he had made into Dodge and groaned inwardly, tried to tell himself that it was all being done for the organization, that if everything did go according to plan, the Halloran gang would be broken and finished before nightfall.

'You the Pinkerton man who wants to travel in this coach?' grunted the driver thickly. His tone implied that he considered no one should have any privileges, and that if he had his way, Hilger would have been forced to wait for the ordinary stage that afternoon.

'That's right.' Hilger nodded. 'You ready to move out?'

'I reckon so. Ain't goin' to be comfortable. We make a pretty fast time and this country can be torture when the heat head rises. That's the reason why the usual stage leaves in the early afternoon.'

'This will suit me fine,' Hilger said, without conviction. He opened the door and climbed inside, settling himself down in the seat, facing the horses. Two men came out of the depot carrying heavy steel boxes which they deposited in the back, then the driver clambered up on to the seat, lifting the reins and holding them loosely in his gnarled fingers.

'Better watch Bill once he hits the desert trail,' said one of the men, thrusting his head inside the window. 'He usually lets her rip and you'll be lucky if you get to the way station in one piece the way he drives.'

'You tend to your business and I'll do mine,' growled Bill from the driver's seat. He uttered a piercing yell and cracked the snake-like lash of the whip over the backs of the four horses standing patiently in the traces. The stage rattled in every seam and bolt as they drove out of the town, turning past the small rail depot and then cutting south-west, away from the gleaming rails that ran due west from the edge of town. The wooden shacks and twin-storeyed houses were left behind them, they passed through an area of dense chaparral, through a stretch of more rocky country and then into the desert. The sun gradually lifted itself over the horizon at their backs and touched the desert with the first red rays of morning. Before long though, as Hilger well knew, the desert would be scorched with a pitiless, fiery glare, hurting to the eye and making every minute a torture of heat and light. He tried to shift his body into a more comfortable position, but it proved to be a vain attempt. The wood ground into his back and shoulders and it seemed that every comfort had been ignored for speed and security.

Three miles out of town the trail suddenly began to twist and turn sharply, winding in and out of the sandy dunes with the tall buttes lifting out of the dreaming face of the desert in great blocks of fluted sandstone, climbing majestically toward the cloudless blue of the sky. The sun rose higher and the heat was beginning to make itself felt.

As the man back at the depot had prophesied, once they were away from the town and among the level country, Bill lashed at the horses, urging them into a faster pace and the stage rattled and swayed precariously from side to side, threatening to topple over at any second. The horses were really forced to lean to it, their feet kicking up the sand, flinging it high into the air. The hard platings of their hoofs struck metallic echoes from the rocky trail-bed under the dust.

Peering from the window, Hilger let his glance range over the whole area of seeable view. The hard-packed strip of sun-baked dust which was called a trail, although to him it had nothing about it to merit such a description, was littered with stones and pieces of rock and each time they hit one of these the stage would buck and jerk dangerously, leaping crazily from the trail, the wooden wheels crunching down again with a thunderous sound that threatened to tear them loose from their axles.

Stark and arid, the landscape that stretched away around them was a vast emptiness of flat, glaring sand, rimmed in the far distance by a shimmering, upthrusting line of sandstone bluffs. Nearer at hand, there was nothing but the clumps of bitter sage with an occasional twisted cactus and a little greasewood. He could see now why there was little need of the posse while driving through this country. From the driver's seat, it would be possible to see the dust cloud lifted by a bunch of riders many miles away and there was nowhere near the trail where a bunch of men could hide in ambush.

Minutes lengthened into an hour. The heat was intense now, the inside of the coach like an oven and every breath that Hilger took was torture to his lungs. He lit a cigarette, drew the smoke down into his lungs. His mouth and throat were dry and wrinkled with the heat and the smoke was not refreshing, tending to burn him rather than give the pleasure he usually got from a cigarette. But he continued to smoke it, aware of the rising tension in his mind that tightened the muscles of his chest and stomach. By now, his body had grown used to the continual up and down motion, combined with the sideways swing of the stage and he was able to ignore the bruises and bumps on his back and legs.

Presently, they came to a point where the

stage trail began its gradual, twisting climb into the hills that divided the stretching flatness of the desert into two unequal halves. At the moment, they had covered perhaps a quarter of the trail across its burned surface.

As the horses lunged forward in the traces, goaded on by an occasional grunt and a crack of the whip from the driver, Bill sank back into his seat, spat a wad of chewed tobacco on to the trail, coughed a little as the dust dragged up by the plunging feet of the horses entered his nostrils, then dug into his hip pocket, pulling out the flat bottle. He paused for a moment with it raised to his lips, teeth ready to draw out the cork, then turned and handed it down to Hilger through the narrow opening.

'Care for a swig?' he asked genially. 'Get's pretty rough from here on all the way to the station about twenty miles ahead. Better wash as much of the trail dust out of your mouth as you can. Once the sun gets up around noon, it's sheer hell out here.'

Hilger hesitated, would have refused, then accepted the bottle, pulled out the cork and let the fiery liquid trickle down his throat after washing it around his mouth once or twice.

The whole of the desert had now taken on a brassy fiery look, sunlight reflected back on both sides, almost as if the sand had been transformed into a mirror that shone back both light and heat into the interior of the stage. Noon came. There were few shadows on the desert now to relieve the terrible glare. Hilger felt the sweat form on his forehead, rolling down his face, mingling with the dust to form irritating streaks along his cheeks. He checked the Derringer he carried under his frock coat, then thrust it back into the small holster.

Seated on the driving box, the driver flicked the long slender whip over the sweat-streaked backs of the straining horses. Already, their flanks were lathered, their backs and shoulders gleaming in the strong sunlight as they hauled the heavy stage over the shifting white alkali on the desert. Now that they were well beyond the bluffs there was dust and more dust; but this was not the yellow-red dust of the first stretch of the Badlands. This was a white, caustic alkali that worked its way into every crevice and fold of a man's skin, burning worse than the heat itself. They were crossing unending miles, flat miles, in which nothing moved and nothing existed to relieve the deadly monotony. Thoroughbraces creaked and groaned as the wheels tried to bite into the soft, shifting surface of the desert where it was difficult for them to obtain any sort grip.

By early afternoon, they were approaching the far edge of the alkali flats and tall bluffs stood out in a haze of blue-purple on the skyline, reaching up into the cloudless, brassy sky. Rubbing the stinging sweat from his eyes, Hilger shaded them against the vicious glare and peered ahead, his mind already alert for trouble. Sweeping the horizon ahead of them in a glance which took in everything, he noticed where the winding trail from the desert led up into the shelving, craggy hills that lifted in front of them. Rocks stood high on either side, the forward sentinels of what was to come and, in places, it seemed that the trail narrowed to such an extent that the coach would be able to scrape through and no more. Beyond this spot, he guessed that although the trail might still be rocky, it would widen out appreciably as they approached the timberline.

'This where we go through the Pass?' he asked, turning.

Without looking down, the driver nodded

his head. There was a faint note of sarcasm in his gruff tone. 'That's right. The way station is five miles in the hills. But you ain't got no call to worry. I've driven this stage along the trail more times than I care to remember and there ain't been any attack by outlaws on it in all that time.'

'That doesn't mean to say we won't bump into some on this trip,' Hilger muttered harshly. 'What about that gang that jumped the train a few days back? If they're still in this part of the territory, they may be lyin' in wait for the stage rather than try for another train.' He paused, then went on: 'The fact that you always travel at the same time must give away the information that you're carrying gold.'

He let his gaze wander from side to side of the narrow pass that loomed up in front of them, the rocky walls crowding in on the trail. The little warning bell at the back of his mind began to ring. It was a signal he had learned, from his past experience, never to ignore. A strange kind of sixth sense that had saved his life on several past occasions.

Bill flicked his whip once more, cracking it loudly over the backs of the straining horses. The echoes rattled back at them eerily from the rocky walls of the canyon as they made their way more slowly along the steep incline, then rolled on with a creaking of springs and braces into the Pass. There were places where the rocks were less than six inches from the sides of the stage, but the driver guided it expertly through so that in spite of this the rocks did not touch them at any point. Sitting back in his seat, Hilger let his pent-up breath go in slow pinches through his nostrils.

Dust rose in an enveloping cloud as they moved through the pass, out into the more open ground and then on into the tall stands of pine and cedar, the wheels rattling and swaying as they jolted over the rough, stony ground, hitting the rocks which littered the trail. At any moment, Hilger expected the stage to overturn and spill them down the side of the treacherous slope, but somehow they held to the trail and less than half an hour later, came out into the wide clearing among the trees. The way station stood facing the trail. It was a long, low-roofed building with a wide corral at one end of it. Beyond the station, the trail continued into the trees, vanishing into the greenness where the sunlight scarcely ever seemed to penetrate.

As he climbed out of the coach, a bunch of

men came out of the station and walked towards them. Hilger recognized Bat Masterton in the lead.

'We saw no sign of trouble as we rode out here,' the other said. He stood with his thumbs hooked inside his belt. 'Not that it means anythin'. They could be waitin' in the hills.'

'If they intend to stop this stage, that's most likely where they will be. You're sure you know what to do?'

'Half of the boys will ride with the stage as usual. The others are to ride with me a short distance behind. If there is any ruckus off in the rocks or in the hills to draw off the posse with the stage, they'll pull out, leavin' only a couple of men behind. That should be enough to tempt this gang out into the open. You're sure you can hold 'em off for five minutes or so until we get to you?'

The driver snorted in disgust. 'If these critters do decide to hit the stage that scattergun of mine up there will take care of 'em,' he said derisively as he gestured towards the driver's box where a shotgun reposed close to the brake.

'Just be sure you know how to handle that, old-timer, said Masterton harshly.

Bill screwed up his mouth under the bushy

whiskers and contemplated the lawman for a moment before replying. 'Listen,' he said indignantly. 'I know you're a fast man with a gun, but I was usin' a rifle and a shotgun before you were born, young fella.' He glared at Bat Masterton for a long moment and then turned on his heel and stumped into the way station.

Masterton glanced after him for a second with a look of grim amusement on his face, then shrugged and turned to the waiting men. Hilger moved on into the station, where there was a welcome coolness after the tremendous heat on the desert. There was a stay of half an hour before the stage moved off again, giving the men a chance to change the horses. The beer was warm and flat and the food unappetising, but after the long, gruelling drive of the morning, it tasted like heaven to Hilger.

The smell of the pines hit them shortly after they moved out again, following the trail deeper into the thick timber. Within minutes the world had become a place of dim green shadows and the sharp aromatic scent. Hilger leaned back in his seat, relishing the cool breeze that somehow found its way in through the open windows. There was no dust here and in places, where a century of pine needles had formed a deep carpet on the trail, there was little sound from the wheels or the hoofs of the horses and they seemed to be driving through a dim world of stillness that was in complete contrast to the nightmare journey through the alkali flats.

Hilger felt confident that the Halloran gang would try to hit the stage before it reached Dodge City; but there was no way of telling when, or where, the attack might come. He took out the Derringer, laid it on his knee. The tension began to lift in his mind, tensing the muscles of his body, making him apprehensive of every little sound off among the trees.

The posse, riding with them on either side, kept their eyes moving, alert for trouble, but they had proceeded for more than five miles through the timber, were moving through more open ground, before trouble showed up; and when it came it was from the rocks that lay to one side of the trail. The sudden burst of firing broke through the stillness like the lash of a whip and, glancing through the window of the jolting stage, Hilger saw the small bunch of men, mounted on their horses, off among the rocks, perhaps three hundred yards away.

More rifle shots rang out and there was the shrill whine of a murderous ricochet that struck the side of the stage and screeched into the distance with the scream of tortured metal.

Two of the men moved closer to the stage while the rest of the posse, whooping loudly at the tops of their voices, swung off the trail and took off after the outlaws. At the same time, Bill whipped the horses, urging them on to an even faster rate.

Sitting forward in his seat, Hilger forced a grim smile as he gripped the Derringer tightly, the knuckles of his fingers standing out under the flesh from the pressure he was exerting. Everything seemed to be going exactly as he had planned back in Dodge. He watched as the posse men vanished in a cloud of rising dust into the rocks after the outlaws. The stage rattled and swayed perilously from side to side as they rolled down the slope, the trail seeming to drop away in front of them at an alarming rate. Grimly, he held on to the door with one hand, steadying himself. If he had guessed right, the rest of that outlaw gang would be waiting for them a little way along the trail, believing that they had only the two posse men to deal with and that the other outlaws would have drawn the rest of the men off sufficiently far to make it impossible for them to get back on to the trail in time to prevent the hold-up.

They rolled through the thin fringe of stunted trees, out into more open ground, flat and featureless. No, Hilger realized, not quite featureless. The outlaws had chosen the spot for their ambush well. There was a small rising column of rock less than a quarter of a mile away and as the stage headed out into the desert, a group of three men burst into view from behind the red sandstone rock and came towards them, spurring their mounts quickly, legs kicking viciously at the flanks of their horses.

The outlaws' mounts would be fresh and Hilger knew that in spite of their own speed, those men would soon catch up with them. He narrowed his eyes against the sunlight that streamed into the stage. At least, he thought with a faint sense of relief, there were only three men for them to contend with and if they could keep them occupied until Bat Masterton and the other bunch of posse men arrived on the scene, the trap would snap shut on the Halloran gang and his work would have been accomplished. For a moment, there was a sense of wild elation in him, but he forced it down, realizing that even now, when it seemed that he was sure to succeed, something could conceivably go wrong and his triumph might be short-lived.

'How are we doin'?' yelled the driver, glancing behind him.

'Just keep drivin' this coach and make sure it stays upright,' Hilger called back. 'They're gaining on us now, but if we can hold 'em off for five minutes, we've got 'em trapped.'

The outlaws came closer. A bullet hit the roof of the stage and whined off the hard metal. Leaning out of the window, Hilger waited until the men had come within range of the tiny weapon he carried, then squeezed off a shot, saw one of the men stagger a little in the saddle as the bullet found its mark in his shoulder, but he still held on grimly to the reins and stayed in the saddle.

The horses hauling the stage continued to pound ahead, throwing up a cloud of dust which swirled around the stage and made it a more difficult target for the oncoming outlaws. Hilger took another swift bead on one of the men, holding the gun steady in both hands as the stage rocked and swayed, cursing a little as the bullet missed its target.

For several moments, the pursuit continued. More shots came from the outlaws as they continued to pump shot after shot at the stage. The two posse men were returning the fire, but it seemed to be having little effect, for the outlaws continued to sweep in on them, fanning out a little now so as to come in from both sides.

Sitting back, Hilger reloaded the Derringer. It was too puny a weapon for long range work and he felt a twinge of irritation that he had not brought a Colt with him, although it would have perhaps made him a little too conspicuous. Whatever else, he had not wanted to arouse any suspicions in Butte Point.

Cautiously, he thrust his head out of the window to throw a quick glance in the direction of the timber at the far edge of the desert. There was still no sign of Bat Masterton and the rest of the posse riding to their help. Grimly, he shaded his eyes against the sunglare, then withdrew his head quickly into the stage as a couple of slugs struck the side of the coach within inches of his skull.

Then, without warning, the driver suddenly uttered a low coughing grunt and slumped forward in the driver's seat, the reins still held in his hands, but slackly now, with little strength holding the plunging, bucking horses. The stage began to career madly along the twisting trail, swaying from side to side.

10

Retribution Bullet

There was not a moment to lose. Knowing that at any second another bullet might hit him, Hilger forced himself to ignore the possibility. Thrusting open the door, he paused for a moment, as the wind whipped at his coat, flapping it painfully around his middle. Then, reaching up, he gripped the roof of the stage and swung himself outward, clinging on for grim death as the violent motion of the stage threatened to hurl him off. His fingers seemed suddenly numb, scarcely able to bear his weight. Gritting his teeth, the thunder of the horses roaring in his ears, the grit and dust clogging his mouth and nostrils until he could hardly breathe, he began to swing his legs in a wide arc. At the same time, he forced himself to keep a tight hold on the roof of the swaying coach, hauling himself up, the muscles of his arms and shoulders cracking with the strain.

For a long moment, he had the sickening feeling that he wasn't going to make it, that his fingers would be forced to release their hold before he could clamber up on to the roof. Sweat began to trickle down his back. God but he had to get up there before the outlaws closed in on them.

With a last despairing effort, he swung himself in a wide arc, managed to get a toehold on the roof and pulled himself up with an effort that almost wrenched his arms from their sockets. For several seconds he could do nothing but lie on top of the roof of the jolting stagecoach, holding on for grim death, sucking air down into his tortured lungs. Gradually, the roaring in his ears began to fade. Pushing himself up on to his arms, he looked about him. The outlaws were still a couple of hundred yards away, but closing in fast and one of the posse men had been hit, was swaying drunkenly in the saddle, blood staining the back of his shirt.

Crawling forward, he lowered himself into the driver's seat, took the reins from the wounded driver and hauled hard on them, forced to exert every ounce of strength to slow the forward run of the horses. Slowly, the stage rolled to a halt. Even before it had come to a standstill, Hilger had released his hold on the reins, had pushed the limp body of the driver to one side and, crouching down behind the upright, grabbed the loaded shotgun from its place near the handbrake.

The outlaws came in, whooping and yelling now that the stage had stopped and Hilger waited tensely until the leading man was less than thirty yards away, before lifting the shotgun and squeezing off one of the triggers. The deadly charge of lead took the man full in the face. He uttered a single, shrill cry, fell back from the saddle as if he had been blasted out of it, his body pumped full of lead, shredded in a score of places. He bounced as he hit the ground, rolling over several times before lying still. The riderless horse plunged wildly away, racing off into the distance.

Gripping the shotgun tightly in his hands, he waited for the other two to come within range, but the men drew off after seeing what had happened to their companion, evidently not wishing to try things with a shotgun, preferring to stay out of range and try to pick Hilger off with rifle and Colt fire.

Bullets hammered a vicious tattoo against the side of the stage as he thrust himself closely against the top of the stage. The horses plunged and kicked, but made no attempt to stampede.

During a brief lull in the firing, a harsh voice from the rocks shouted, 'Better throw down those guns and lift your hands, or we'll kill you all.'

Hilger said nothing. He could feel the tension building up and tried to spot any movement where the two outlaws had swung down from their horses, diving for cover. The longer he could force them to stay there and keep their heads down, the better chance there was of Masterton and the others arriving on the scene in time to prevent the two men from grabbing their horses and riding out, giving up the attempt to rob the stage. If it was Ross Halloran out there, it would go against the grain for him to leave without getting his hands on the gold they were carrying, but even he would not be so foolhardy as to try to fight it out with a large bunch of men, particularly if he discovered that Bat Masterton was leading them.

'I'm giving you ten seconds,' called the harsh voice again. 'If you ain't thrown down your guns by then, you're finished.'

'Why don't you try to come and get us, Halloran,' Hilger yelled.

There was a long pause, then the voice called: 'How'd you know my name, mister?'

Hilger grinned. In spite of the danger, he had to keep the other there. 'You don't know me, Halloran, but I've been hunting you down for more than six months now, ever since you helped yourself to the gold on the Abilene express.'

'You one of those Pinkerton men?'

'That's right. The name is Hilger.'

Dimly, Hilger heard the second man with Halloran mutter something in a low, urgent voice, but the words did not carry to him. Then, out of the corner of his eye, he caught the sudden movement in the distance, swung his head and saw the posse ride out of the trees. In the same second, the man with Halloran cried: 'It's a trap, Ross. I told you it was!'

Lifting his head slightly, Hilger saw the two figures dart out from behind the rocks less than a hundred yards away. Swiftly, he raised the shotgun to his shoulder as they ran for their horses, swinging themselves swiftly into the saddle. The gun boomed loudly in his ears as he sent the last charge of shot after them, cursed savagely under his breath as it missed. Getting to his feet, he waved an urgent arm in the direction of the posse, saw them swerve as they glimpsed the two men racing off into the distance.

A fusillade of shots rang out as the posse began their chase of the fleeing men and Hilger was forced to watch helplessly, knowing that there was nothing he could do about it now. There was a feeling of anger deep within him. If Halloran slipped through his fingers now after all of his careful planning, all of the patience, the long waiting, just to set up this trap.

He stared off into the distance, trying to probe through the cloud of dust that lifted around the bunch of riders spurring their horses towards the timber that grew along the edge of the desert.

Beside him, the driver suddenly stirred, moaned deep in his throat as the pain of his wound brought him back to consciousness. Hilger gently eased the other over on to his back. The oldster's face was grey behind the beard and the red stain on the back of his shirt had grown a little wider during the past few minutes. Hilger knew that the chances were he was bleeding internally and that unless they got him to a doctor soon, he would certainly die.

The two posse men who had accompanied the stage swung back into their saddles. The man who had been hit held his injured arm across his chest and there was blood dripping from his wrist, but in answer to Hilger's question, he indicated that he was still able to ride.

'Help me get the driver inside the coach,' he muttered, clambering down to the ground. 'We'll have to run on into Dodge as quickly as we can if he's to have any chance at all.'

'Sure, sure,' muttered the other. There was sweat on his face, running in tiny rivulets down his cheeks and a lot of it was not due to the heat of the sun, Hilger reckoned. But the other helped him willingly enough, heaving the old man's legs from the ground and backing with him gently to the steps leading up into the stage. Laying him carefully on the seat, the posse man said: 'You want to stay here and look after him while I drive the stage, Mister Hilger?'

Hilger considered that and nodded almost at once. 'Get us there as fast as you can,' he said sharply. 'And don't stop for anything.'

'I won't,' promised the other. A few moments later he had climbed up on to the driver's seat, had cracked the whip over the patiently waiting horses and they were moving out, rattling over the dusty ribbon of the trail.

Dim purple shadows were beginning to lie over the low hills as they rode down into Dodge. The sun dropped behind the hills like a red penny going into a black box, leaving only the vivid explosion of reds and oranges across the western horizon to indicate where it had set. For most of the journey, the driver had lain unconscious on the seat opposite Hilger, only occasionally rousing himself, muttering something under his breath which Hilger could not make out. He did not seem to be suffering much pain now which was, as Hilger recognized, a bad sign.

Presently, they drove on to a broad trail which wound its way through lush green meadows that opened up on either side, crossed the wooden bridge that spanned the narrow creek and rode into the dusty main street of Dodge City.

The posse man drove the stage past the hotel, the saloon and sheriff's office and didn't stop until they were level with the depot. He jumped down just as Hilger opened the door and got out.

A couple of men came hurrying out of the depot, running towards the stage. Evidently the fact that they were fifteen minutes behind schedule had made them convinced that something had happened.

'Get Doc Adams,' the posse man said harshly. 'We were hit by those outlaws. Bill has been hit pretty bad.'

One of the men ran off along the street without stopping to ask any further questions. He came back less than three minutes later, with a tall, thin faced man wearing a pointed goatee.

The doctor climbed inside the stage to make his initial examination, was less than a couple of minutes before climbing out again. 'I want a couple of you men to help carry him out and up to my office,' he ordered, 'This bullet has got to come out.'

'You reckon he's goin' to be all right, Doc?' asked the posse man.

'Hard to say right now,' muttered the other non-committally. 'He's lost a deal of blood and that long journey hasn't helped much. In fact, if it wasn't that he's got an iron constitution, I'd say his chances were pretty goddamned slender.'

Hilger waited until the driver had been carried along the street, then turned to find Wyatt Earp standing beside him.

'Was it the Halloran gang?' asked the other pointedly.

Hilger nodded slowly. 'Halloran was there with the others,' he replied. 'They shot the driver soon after they ambushed us. Fortunately, Masterton came on the scene in time, but the last I saw of them, Halloran and one of the others was riding out hell for leather.'

'Bat and the boys will get 'em,' Earp said with conviction. 'They should be back in town within the hour.' He looked round at the stage where the men were lifting down the gold. 'Why don't you get yourself a drink and a bite to eat, Mister Hilger? There's nothin' you can do until the boys get back with news of Halloran.'

Hilger nodded his head wearily. There was a lot of truth in what the other said. Slowly, he made his way along the street towards the hotel.

It was two hours later before Bat Masterton and the posse rode into Dodge City. Hilger heard them ride in and went out into the street, waited until the posse had dispersed, moving towards the hotel and saloons, before going over to the sheriff's office. Wyatt Earp's smile was tight and hard, did not touch his eyes as he gestured the Pinkerton man to a chair. Masterton stood by the wall, his face emotionless.

'Well?' demanded Hilger as the silence dragged on, 'what happened. Did you get those killers?'

'We got them all except Halloran,' Masterton said sombrely. His gaze locked with Hilger's. 'But I don't reckon he'll get far. Those two men who drew off the posse were soon run to earth. They put up a good fight, but we killed 'em both. The same went for the man who rode off with Halloran when we appeared on the scene. We brought his body back with us. His name was Blade Wisherton accordin' to the information we have, although like most of the others he probably has more names than we'll ever discover.'

'And Ross Halloran? What about him?'

'He's badly wounded. We lost him in the thickets, but if he ain't dead by now, he sure will be before mornin'. There must be more'n a dozen slugs in him.'

Hilger sat back in his chair, staring straight ahead of him, not seeing either of the two men in the room with him. Was that the end of Ross Halloran? he wondered tightly. Could he write him off? Could he say that his job was finished, that the West had heard the last of one of the greatest outlaws it had known? He felt a sense of emptiness deep within him, an uneasy feeling of leaving something half-finished. It was an experience he did not like. He was the kind of man who hated to leave knots untied, stray ends poking out here and there. His was a tidy mind, used to having everything stacked away in neat little piles.

'We spent more'n an hour scouring those thickets for him,' Bat Masterton was saying. 'But there was no sign of him. My guess is that he's still there, dead some place. It's just the sort of end I'd have wished for him myself.'

'If we could only be absolutely certain that he's dead and my job is finished.'

The other shrugged. 'If you'd seen him as I did, you'd believe that he's dead, just as I do,' he said, his tone carrying conviction. 'He won't dare to go anywhere to get his injuries treated and unless he does get medical attention before mornin', then he'll die as sure as anythin'.'

Hilger rubbed his chin with his fingers. He wanted to believe what the other said, but he had the strange feeling that all his life, he would be nagged by the question: Was Ross Halloran alive or dead? Had he been killed up there on the edge of the desert, or had he somehow survived to spend his ill-gotten gains somewhere south of the Border where the law could not touch him?

Slowly, his face corroded with pain, blood soaking from his chest and shoulder, Ross Halloran crawled on his hands and knees to the edge of the clearing, where the dense bushes hemmed him in. His hat lay on the ground beside him and his face was white and glistening with sweat. The pain was deep inside him, burning along his ribs and he felt weak and dizzy, a sick sensation in the pit of his stomach. His horse had run on somewhere into the thorn thickets that grew thickly in this area, but that, more than anything else, had saved his life. He had lain, only half conscious, on the moist earth, listening to the reckless flight of his horse as it crashed its way through the undergrowth, the steady tattoo of its hooves fading swiftly into the distance.

Then, close on its heels, there came the sound of the posse as they crowded in on him, shouting and yelling in their excitement.

They had stamped through the brush within two feet of him, but had somehow missed seeing him lying there, so weak from the pain and loss of blood that he had been unable to lift his gun and would have had no chance at all of defending himself if he had been discovered.

Listening to the crashing of boots and hoofs through the thicket, it came to him then that he had overplayed his hand, that this man Hilger, the Pinkerton agent who had been trailing him all these months, had finally proved to be too clever for him. He wondered briefly how long the other had been planning the trap which had snapped shut, catching him completely unawares only a few minutes before.

If only he had listened to Dane and the others, and had pulled out for the Mexico border while they had had the chance. But it had seemed to be so absolutely certain that no one in the territory would expect them to strike in the same part of the territory and so soon after their last holdup. Maybe if it had been left to Wyatt Earp and Bat Masterton, his reasoning would have been correct. But he had failed to consider the possibilty that this Pinkerton agent might be in town and it had been that which had proved to be his undoing.

The posse had beaten the brush all around the spot where he had lain hidden, but the fates had been kind and after a while they had ridden back, taking with them Blade's body. How long he had been lying there since they had pulled out, he did not know. But several times, he had drifted off into unconsciousness only to come round, shivering with cold and fever. Now, at last, he was fully conscious. The stars were visible above his head, shining brilliantly in the dark black of the night sky and there was an icily cold wind blowing through the thickets, stirring the dry, stiff branches with an eerie sound, cracking and moaning like the voices of the dead, sighing over this barren land.

He knew that he could not afford to remain where he was, that somehow he had to move, try to get to a doctor. Once his wounds were tended to, he might be able to move on out, get himself a horse and ride for the border. There was money in plenty up at the old prospector's shack now and only himself to get it, unless Dane and Monroe had been more fortunate and had escaped from the men they had drawn off from watching the stage.

It was not going to be easy, even if he

made it to a town. Word would undoubtedly have been spread about him, warning everyone to be on the look out for him. They would not even have to give his description, merely to say that he had been wounded. Nevertheless, it was a risk he would have to take. He knew, deep within himself, that he was badly hurt, bleeding from several wounds, and he did not dare think about how many pieces of lead might be inside him. But so long as he was alive and able to move, he had to keep on going, all through the night if necessary. It was possible that the posse might return to continue the search at dawn, especially if the Pinkerton man figured that he might still be alive. Earp and Masterton might be willing to leave things as they were, convinced that no further effort to find him was necessary. But not Hilger. Like a bulldog, he would never let go until he was absolutely certain that Ross Halloran was dead.

A red wall of agony fogged his eyes, forcing a low moan past his tightly clenched teeth as he continued to thrust himself forward. He dashed his hand across his eyes, wiping away the sweat that threatened to blind him. A dim bush lay ahead of him and he blundered into it, lacking the strength to move to one side. Thorns raked and scratched his hands and face and there were long tears in his clothing. But the pain of the deep scratches kept him conscious, made it possible for him to keep crawling forward on hands and knees.

The moon came out an unguessable time later and he was able to see a little more clearly where he was going. Gradually, the thickets thinned, the ground became more stony. Sometime after midnight, he came to a stream that ran swiftly down the side of the hill and he did his best to wash and bathe his wounds. The cold water shocked a little of the life back into him. Sucking air down into his lungs, he drank his fill of the water, rested for a little while, and then, somehow, incredibly, succeeded in getting to his feet, staggering like a drunken man from side to side, weaving blindly as he strove to remain upright.

The blood pounded and throbbed at the back of his temples and apart from this, sounds seemed to be coming as if from a great distance. More frequently now, he was forced to rest and the conviction grew in his mind, in spite of everything he had hoped to the contrary, that he was not going to make it.

A narrow gully showed ahead of him, and he crawled into it, sinking down on to the hard, rocky floor. The darkness of unconsciousness came to him again, overwhelming him. When he finally came round again, his body bitterly cold and stiff, with dried blood congealed on his skin his shirt sticking to his flesh, it was grey dawn. He lay for a long moment, staring up at the greying sky, unable to summon up sufficient strength to move. Gradually, a little life seeped back into his frozen body. With a tremendous effort, knowing that he was running the risk of reopening his wounds and starting the bleeding again, he pushed himself up on to his haunches, staring about him. Rocks lay on all sides and he realized that he had somehow stumbled on to one of the wide ledges that ran along the lee of the hills.

Sobbing air down into his tortured chest, he rubbed the stubble on his chin as he lifted his head a little, staring about him. Then he stiffened, reaching down for the gun, in his holster, his fingers closing tightly around it. There was a sudden movement off to his right, the unmistakable sound of a horse moving forward. Gently, he eased the gun from its holster, prepared to sell his life dearly if this was one of the posse come back to try to find him, probably determined to collect the reward that was out for him, dead or alive.

A moment later, through the shaking red haze that wavered in front of his eyes, he saw the horse move out from the rocks and halt twenty feet away from the end of the gully. Several seconds fled before it came to him that this was his own mount, that somehow their paths had crossed again. The realization brought a little strength and determination back into his body. Now, if he could only get the horse to him and climb up into the saddle, he had a chance. A slender one, it was true, but a chance nevertheless.

Somehow, he got to his feet, edged his way forward very slowly, careful not to spook the animal. Once the horse took it into its head to gallop off, he would never catch it. As he drew nearer to it, he began to call it softly by name. He saw its head come up as it looked in his direction. Then it tossed its head sharply and his heart leapt hammering into his chest as he started forward, expecting it to move away from him. But it remained standing where it was, head moving up and down, letting him come right up to it. He put out his hand and stroked its neck, soothing it, feeling it tremble a little under his hand.

'It's all right now, boy,' he said softly. 'Nothin' is goin' to happen now.'

It stood quite still as he moved around it, striving to get his foot into the stirrup. Even when he succeeded, he still had to pull himself up into the saddle and stay there. Sucking air down into his lungs, he held his breath for a moment, then let it go with an explosive whoosh, gripped the reins tightly and lifted himself up.

There was fresh blood on the front of his shirt as he forced himself upright in the saddle. For a moment, the rocks in the grey dawn light swayed and tilted in front of his vision and he almost fell again. Not until five minutes later was he able to touch spurs to the horse's flanks and let it pick its own way forward through the rocks, pointing it downgrade.

The sun came up when he was still in the foothills and the heat head began to intensify as he rode out on to the wide plain, found the narrow tram that wound over the prairie and followed it, content to let the horse have its head.

The morning passed slowly, the minutes dragging themselves by in a nightmare of heat and pain and weakness. He met no one on the trail and it was an hour after high noon when he saw the small settlement directly ahead of him, the dull smudge of the buildings wavering in the heat haze.

Halloran hesitated only briefly. He checked the Colt at his waist, then pouched the weapon, straightened himself as much as possible in the saddle and rode along the narrow street that ran through the middle of the small town. There were a few curious stares following him, but nobody made a move in his direction and he continued to ride until he saw the sign outside the doctor's office.

Biting his lips as agony flooded through him, he forced himself to dismount and walk steadily up to the boardwalk and into the office, without bothering to knock.

The man seated behind the small desk, looked up sharply as he entered, then scraped back his chair and got quickly to his feet, his mouth hanging slackly open.

'Just keep quiet and nothin' is goin' to happen,' Ross said harshly.

'Who are you?' demanded the other, his eyes riveted on the gun in Ross's hand. Then his eyes narrowed a little and a look of realization came to his face. 'You're Ross Halloran, the outlaw.'

'That's right,' Ross nodded. 'Guess that news travels fast in this part of the territory. I came here because you're goin' to take some lead out of me and also patch up these wounds.'

'What makes you think that I'll help you,' muttered the other. 'If you shoot me you'll die anyway because there's nobody else within fifty miles who can get those bullets out of you.'

Ross forced a grim smile. 'I didn't ride into town alone,' he lied. 'There are two of my men outside. If you don't do exactly as I say and if I don't appear out in the street within half an hour, they'll take a couple of hostages and shoot them down. Now make up your mind fast. Are you goin' to do as I say, or do you want to condemn two innocent people to death.'

He saw the sudden look of indecision on the doctor's face, knew that even if the other thought he was lying, it was something he would never dare to risk.

'Very well.' The doctor's shoulders slumped fractionally as he realized that he was beaten. 'I'll do it. But it will make very little difference in the long term.'

'Just get this lead out of me and hurry,' Ross snapped.

Exactly half an hour later, with pain lancing through his body, Ross staggered from the couch and forced his blurred vision to concentrate on the doctor's face. The other wiped his hands on the white towel, then said quietly, with conviction. 'Like I said before I started, Halloran, this is not going to make the slightest bit of difference. I've seen gunmen who've been brought in here for me to extract lead from their bodies and I reckon I can tell how badly a man is hurt inside, where it really counts. You've lost a lot of blood, but my guess is that you're losing more inside where I can do nothin' to stop it. If you were to go into one of the hospitals, maybe in Dodge or even further east, then there's a damned good chance that you'll live. But if you mean to ride out of here and keep on riding, then you can take my word for it that you'll be dead in a few days.'

'That won't be any concern of yours, doctor,' Ross said thinly. 'Now turn your back to the wall.'

The other hesitated. With a barely perceptible movement, Ross shifted the gun muzzle until it pointed at the other's stomach. 'I'll give you until three,' he said harshly.

The doctor hesitated only briefly, then turned his face towards the far wall. He dropped without a moan as the butt of Ross's gun struck him on the side of the head just behind the right ear. Taking the key from inside the door, Ross stepped out into the street, locked the door, then thrust the key into his pocket. He reckoned that this strategem ought to keep the doctor from sending a posse out after him for a few hours, long enough for him to get clear of the place.

An early moon saw a single horseman riding slowly south – south for Texas and then beyond, down into the safety of Mexico. He had visited the shack up in the hills for the last time, taken as much of the gold as he had been able to carry, loading it into a single sack which was now tied to his saddle.

As he rode, he kept turning over in his mind the words which the doctor in that small settlement had said. He couldn't possibly live, not with these holes in his body and a possible internal haemorrhage that was draining away his life's blood inside him where he could not stop it. But the determination was there, the belief that he could make it if only he had the will.

Whether it was that the doctor had been more skilful than he knew, or there had been no internal haemorrhage in the first place, it was difficult to tell, but as the days passed and he continued his long journey south, some of the strength flowed back into his body. The wounds began to heal and the fever which had been in his body the first night out, left him and he could think clearly once more.

He rode south, through ghost towns which had been deserted since before the war. He moved off the main trails whenever he smelled smoke or a cooking fire, watching for tracks and idly speculating on the number of unwanted men who must have been living in these wild and desolate parts, wondering at times if Kirby Hilger was still on his trail or whether he had gone back east, firmly believing, as Earp and Masterton most likely did, that he was dead, his body lying somewhere in that thicket far to the north.

There were a thousand places for men to lose themselves in this vast territory, but for Ross Halloran, there was the knowledge that only in Mexico would he ever be really safe.

A week, and then ten days, and he finally came to a trail that twisted and wound through tall timber, along the edge of a wild mountain chain. Here, the sun shone brilliantly as he rode along the edge of the deep canyon, at the bottom of which the waters of the wide river ran sluggishly through the steep rocky sides. He recalled the day when he had last ridden this trail, riding home from the wars in a grey uniform, the uniform of a defeated Army. Another three days at the most, and he would be safely over the border and into Mexico.

He forded the river, aware of the familiar landmarks which opened up all around him. This was the country he had known long before there had been any war, when to be alive had been the greatest experience a man could know. Each day had been a fresh adventure, full of new trails to follow, new things to know and learn. But so much had happened in the past few years that all of these memories now seemed to have happened to someone else and not to him. Whenever he looked back on them, he seemed to be seeing them through the eyes of a stranger.

When he came to the narrow trail which

led through the pass and on to the Halloran spread, he knew that he ought to keep on riding, that he should not turn off, but the desire to see for himself what had happened there in the time he had been away proved to be too strong for him. Slowly, half-fearful of what he might find, he rode across the meadows until he came within sight of the ranch house.

Riding into the dusty courtyard, he reined up, sat forward in the saddle, staring about him in stunned surprise. The barn was a burnt-out wreck of a building. The house itself seemed to have been abandoned for a long time. Weeds grew at the edge of the courtyard and thrust their slender green stems up between the boards of the porch. One of the wooden shutters hung lop-sidedly from twisted hinges.

Slowly, a little warmth crept back into his body. The Northern carpetbaggers had won. He felt the growing bitterness in his mind. Somehow, they had finally forced his mother out of the ranch, had let it fall into decay rather than take it over themselves. He tightened his lips, gritting his teeth until the muscles of his jaw lumped painfully under his flesh. Damn them, he thought fiercely. Damn them all.

He lifted the reins, made to pull round his mount's head, to ride out of the dusty courtyard and put the memory of this place behind him for good. Then, without warning, the door of the ranch house opened with the audible squeal of rusted metal. He narrowed his eyes against the glare of the sunlight as he leaned forward in the saddle in an attempt to make out who it was stood there.

'That you, Faro?' he called, straining to see.

For a moment there was no answer, and then a voice that he only vaguely remembered, one he had heard only once, said: 'I always figured that you had the nine lives of a cat, Halloran, and that if you did manage to escape, you might come back here eventually.'

Kirby Hilger stepped down from the porch. There was a small snub-nosed Derringer in his right hand and it was levelled, as steady as a rock, on Ross's chest. 'Seems that this is the end of the trail as far as you're concerned.'

'If you think that you're takin' me in, Hilger, you're wrong,' Ross said tersely.

'Makes no difference to me if you ride back or go over the saddle of your horse,' said the other evenly. 'But this time, I don't intend to let you slip through my fingers. We got all of the others. You're the only one still–'

Ross moved suddenly. His right hand struck downward for the gun in its holster. His fingers closed around the smooth butt, jerking it free. But the loss of blood and the weakness of his wounds had slowed what had once been one of the fastest draws in the west. The muzzle of the gun was just clear of leather when Hilger fired. The Derringer made only a faint sound as he squeezed the trigger, but the bullet found its mark.

Ross Halloran reeled drunkenly in the saddle as he fought to hold life in his eyes. Then a faint look of bewilderment spread over his face as he slipped from the saddle. As he fell, his weight caught the rope holding the sack to the saddle, breaking it loose. Hilger went forward slowly, stood looking down at the dead man who lay in the dust, the gold coins spilled all over him, gleaming yellowly in the flooding sunlight.

The publishers hope that this book has given you enjoyable reading. Large Print Books are especially designed to be as easy to see and hold as possible. If you wish a complete list of our books please ask at your local library or write directly to:

Dales Large Print Books
Magna House, Long Preston,
Skipton, North Yorkshire.
BD23 4ND

This Large Print Book, for people
who cannot read normal print,
is published under the auspices of

THE ULVERSCROFT FOUNDATION

... we hope you have enjoyed this book.
Please think for a moment about those
who have worse eyesight than you ...
and are unable to even read or enjoy
Large Print without great difficulty.

You can help them by sending a
donation, large or small, to:

**The Ulverscroft Foundation,
1, The Green, Bradgate Road,
Anstey, Leicestershire, LE7 7FU,
England.**
or request a copy of our brochure for
more details.

The Foundation will use all donations
to assist those people who are visually
impaired and need special attention
with medical research, diagnosis
and treatment.

Thank you very much for your help.